MW01277203

The Lives of

La Escondida

a novel by

Carolyn Kingson

Published in the USA by Lirio Publications

Box 113

Dixon, New Mexico 87527

Cover Art by Gayle fulwyler Smith

Author Photo by Douglas Fir

ISBN-13: 978-0615485782 (Lirio Publications)

ISBN-10: 0615485782

For Chippy

The Lives of

La Escondida

One

Javier kept to the edge of the crowd near the food stalls, trying to blend with the rabble that had come to view the spectacular humiliation of his family. Though he wore ragged white cotton pants and shirt, and a disintegrating sombrero on his bowed head— peasant garb borrowed from the gardener at his parents' grand home—any close inspection would have shown his skin to be white and smooth and his features devoid of indigenous ancestry. His stomach was knotted from fear and the greasy smell of roasting corn, but he was trying to stand his ground here outside the plaza where other smoke, infinitely more horrible, would soon rise.

Javier's father, whether cowardly or brave, was upholding family honor by his attendance at the *auto de fé*. Erstwhile friends—all the adult Spanish males of Mexico City were present—glanced surreptitiously at his impassive face as he stared straight toward the altar. The men had been standing in the relentless sun for nearly three hours; it could not be long before the culmination of the ceremony when Fortunato Rodriguez de Matos y Andrade, the father-in-law of the stoic watcher, would make his public penance and be put to death by the Holy Office of the Inquisition.

The young man hiding in gardener's clothing could see all too well into the plaza in front of the palace of the Holy Office. A stage had been raised for the crowd to watch and learn the consequences of apostasy to the Holy Faith. Held aloft by silver posts, a tasseled canopy covered an altar laden with gold implements—candelabra, chalice, monstrance, lectern. Behind it were high-backed thrones and a row of magnificent staves depicting the crook of St Peter, the Lamb of God and the Sacred Heart. Princes of the church, with their heavy jowls and cold eyes, stood and kneeled, exhorted and declaimed, kissed and raised the tome containing the Word of God as their diamond-encrusted miters and embroidered, bejeweled vestments shimmered and flashed.

The Castilians in the audience also stood and

kneeled, reciting declarations of faith and prayers in unison. Surely some were aghast or in terror; surely many would have absented themselves if they could, but all were powerless before the absolute authority of the Holy Office. Javier's grandfather sat slumped on a low stool wearing white robes and a cone-shaped hat. His grandson shut his eyes as soon as he recognized the old man.

Accused of being a Jew who had reverted to the faith his family had abjured in Spain, Fortunato was now to pay the price for his acquiescence to the charge. It had come after torture so dreadful there was nothing to which he would not have confessed, but it was nevertheless true. The pain had also induced him to recant and proclaim once more his devotion to Christianity, thus he had been granted death by strangulation before his body was burned. Javier knew he could not bear to remain for those terrible events, but had wanted to stay as long as he could, so that, in however inaudible a voice, someone was saying prayers for the kind old man's soul. This he was doing, standing shoulder to shoulder with the gaping Indians.

The reek of singed corn would forever after make him ill.

~~~~~~~

From seat 14F, Andorra watched as the Manzano Mountains dropped abruptly to treeless flats. She nodded absently to her talkative seatmate as she felt the beginning of the turn, the decrease in speed and the precipitous descent to the Albuquerque airport. The man next to her had been trying to ingratiate himself all the way from Dallas. She had learned he was a physicist at the Los Alamos Laboratory, had recently bought a foreclosed house at sixty percent of what had been asked the year before, played bass in a jazz combo and had hiked the Inca Trail. Also that he was single. Andorra was used to this. She was beautiful and men could not resist preening and strutting around her. Squeezed between him and the skin of an airplane at 38,000 feet, she presented an opportunity he could not pass up.

He had been too busy making his play to notice that he'd learned next to nothing about her. She had traveled from the UK. Yes, her accent was English. He loved English accents, as it happened. She had family north of Santa Fe. That was of interest—Los Alamos, where he was going, was north of Santa Fe—but her trip would be brief and she had many obligations; thank you, but she wouldn't be able to squeeze in dinner. She had smiled politely and returned to the window.

This was nearly the final leg of a trip Andorra

had been anticipating for a long time. For almost two years a rosewood box in the overhead bin had been waiting on the sideboard in her London flat. Now that school was over with exams passed and thesis defended, the time had come. It was true that it wasn't to be a long trip. She had research to do in Albuquerque and Santa Fe in the State Historical Library, the museums and archives—visits essential to the book she hoped to write about the Spanish Conquest in New Mexico. But there was more. The box contained her father's ashes and she was carrying it to that special place where he belonged.

Hours and time zones earlier she had begun her trip at Heathrow. The familiar airport process, the special hassle of flying to the United States, the visions of New Mexico and of her father—not waiting for her this time, not waiting for her ever again—all this had occupied her thoughts, triggered memories and reminded her of the first independent achievement of her life. Andorra could still see the day she had asked her mother for permission to visit her father. She still wondered where she had found the courage since mention of him was the surest way to bring her mother's wrath, but she had no longer known if she would recognize his face. What if she were to forget his face? Her cherished memories of his love and care, her imaginary escape when things were scary—she had feared those refuges were perilously close to slipping away.

Her mother had been sitting in a delicate chair on the terrace, her long, slim legs arranged to advantage, her hair in a smooth, blond twist. Was it in Italy? Austria? Switzerland? Andorra remembered how it had felt to be gangly, painfully awkward and afraid. She also remembered her mother slamming down her wine glass and looking at her with a contempt that made her cringe.

"For God's sake, Andorra, why do you want to go back to that wasteland?" She raised her glass and emptied it so rapidly that wine flowed past her mouth and fell on her silk jacket. "Look what you made me do!" She scanned the terrace for the waiter as she dabbed at the stain with a napkin. "And your father! What does he have to offer you? Of all the cultureless, miserable... Where *is* that waiter?"

She had been ready with her argument. A new friend of her mother's had offered to take them to Kashmir for a stay on a houseboat. Andorra knew her mother was very interested in him—and his money— and she'd overheard him asking if there were other family the child could stay with.

"I don't want to go on that houseboat, Mummy. I hate India…and aren't houseboats rather small?" She had seen her mother get a look in her eye as a new thought made it past her mental barricades and, albeit with the knowledge that her mother was glad to be rid of her, she'd achieved her visit to New Mexico, and another every year until three years ago. Sometimes the trip began at Heathrow; sometimes it had originated in Madrid or Paris, whatever the closest international airport to her mother's always-temporary home. The flight would land in Dallas, Atlanta or Los Angeles and continue on to Albuquerque, where Papi, standing tall and bulky, handsome and rugged in jeans and work shirt, would be waiting. They would make their way north, first by interstate, then by state and county roads in Papi's pick-up, climbing alongside the Rio Grande and its tributary, the Rio Oscuro—sustainers of life in that lovely, dry land—and at the end, up the arroyo on horseback to the old adobe house waiting for her in the meadow. La Escondida. The Hidden Place.

Worlds away from the majesty and grime of Europe, the simple house made from earth and pine was her birthplace and early childhood playground. She and Papi had loved the old house as they loved each other; not so, her English mother. Why couldn't she have abandoned me along with Papi, Andorra wondered again? What sort of perverse motherly instinct held tight to a child only to undercut her confidence and spirit?

Papi—Aaron Sandoval—had been a rancher. He'd owned hundreds of acres and held leases on public lands that went on forever. He'd moved the cattle from pasture to pasture, assisted with their births, saved them from snowstorms and delivered them to market. He'd repaired barns, strung fences and maintained family ties. More than one wayward boy from town had found a steadying start on a better path with Aaron's support and a summer job on the ranch. In fact, the summers had done the same for Andorra.

She had now been without him for two years. In the year before he died she had been called by his cousin, Adelina Sandoval, to come to his aid. He'd had a stroke. She had found him disheveled, confused and surprisingly content to leave his remote home and return with her to England. The worst sign of all: he was willing to leave. He had padded around her flat, staring out the windows, usually in foggy silence, though there also had been painful moments when he tried to communicate. Andorra winced at the memory. After eight months he had passed away in his sleep. Only seventy. Anyone who knew him would have imagined

Aaron raging against the dying of the light but he had faded like a wisp of smoke.

Now at twenty-seven, Andorra's early awkwardness had turned to grace. Her shoulder-length hair was dark and hung in waves and curls; brown eyes from her father looked darker yet contrasted with the delicate skin tones she had inherited from her mother; her hips were full and her waist was slim. She seemed entirely too beautiful to be living, as she did, with only a cat for company but she felt, and feared, it was her natural state. She had looked at her parents' example and concluded that partnership was too often a nightmare of thwarted and crushed hopes. Her last boyfriend had been a disaster. Better to stick to other people's history.

There was no hint from the plane's window of the September beauty that awaited her at home. Asters would be scattered in the cool grass around the spring; cottonwoods by the arroyo and aspens above the house would be starting to turn. She thought of a favorite poem: "My aspens dear, whose airy cages quelled, quelled or quenched in leaves the leaping sun..." and imagined sunlight glancing through the leaves like diamonds playing catch-me-if-you-can. She saw water sliding over the image on the boulder near the spring as she and her father wet the petroglyph to make the picture stand out. Indians had hit stone on stone to make spirals, battle scenes and humpbacked flute players; rocks with these and other drawings were all over the hills—pale lines on dark basalt—but theirs didn't resemble any of them. It looked something like Frosty the Snowman, they'd joked, with a round, wide-brimmed hat on two circles. She could remember how her father had tried so painfully in his last days to tell her something about the rock. That was where she was going to bury his ashes. She had understood him, no matter how blurred the words. It was what he had wanted. They had always understood each other.

Andorra looked remarkably un-rumpled in her short, aubergine jacket and navy skirt as she made polite conversation with the physicist at the baggage carousel. He insisted on hauling her suitcase from the conveyer to the floor; she thanked him, assured him that it had all been "a pleasure," and said goodbye. He turned in disappointment toward Short-Term Parking while she made her way to Car Rental, and in a moment, he was forgotten. When the car's paperwork was done, her suitcase placed in the trunk and the rosewood box in its carry-on tote on the seat beside her, Andorra headed to the interstate. The Spanish Conquest would wait; first, she was going north to lay Papi to rest. An hour to Santa Fe and a little more beyond.

The ancient gouges of erosion and recent road cuts on either side of the highway exposed earth colored red, ocher, white, gray and lavender. Midnight-green piñons and junipers—pines and cedars—scattered themselves over the pale hills and lined up shoulder to shoulder where runoff watered denser growth. She loved to see this familiar landscape as a child loves the hundredth reading of a favorite book.

North of Santa Fe, she passed Indian Pueblos now revitalized, if you could call it that, with gambling casinos. The Rio Grande, at first far off to the left, approached and met the highway, bringing with it Russian olives, willows and the colossal cottonwoods, which as she had hoped, showed the first touches of blemishless gold. Sunflowers lined the road and her longed-for purple asters massed beneath them.

At last Andorra reached the village of Estancia. Her heart leapt to see that almost nothing had changed: adobe houses covered in pastel stucco, old cottonwoods shading the lanes, orchards of apple, peach and apricot. A building for the volunteer fire department was the only incongruous structure on the main road. She passed the house of Porfirio Sandoval, now his son Joe's.

Bikes were in the bare yard—the boys must be getting big. Next to it was the house where her father's sister, Aunt Lydia, had lived until she died of cancer just before Papi had his first stroke and where Uncle Joe tended his collection of antique farm implements. Their daughter's house with its glassed-in sunroom was on the other side of the highway. Andorra could have recited the history of each dwelling, looped as they were with the skeins of family. Down a side lane, she saw Adelina's house, her destination, and then Adelina herself, hanging clothes in the yard.

At first, the old woman squinted at the strange car entering the driveway but soon was crying, "*¡Mijita!*" and holding tight to her cousin's daughter. Andorra stooped down to kiss the tiny, gray-haired woman and hugged her tight.

"Thank you again, my child, for your letters about Aaron." Adelina spoke Spanish, the language of love and family in Estancia. English was for the outside world. "*El te queria mucho, mijita.*" He loved you so much. "I had much happiness that he could be with you during his last days."

Andorra slipped easily into Spanish. "I feel it too, Auntie, but I can bear it better because I could care for him. He always was kind. He never troubled me."

"Who would believe it?" Adelina laughed. "Here he always troubled us."

"Let me help you with the clothes," Andorra said, leading the way to the line and the basket. "The air smells so good! I am so happy to be here."

"Of course you are content! I made posole for you and apple pie. Oh, what thing better than to have you here. Was it a good trip?" They chatted as the clothes were hung. "Come in and see my new refrigerator. She makes ice by herself! Let's have a Coke."

The refrigerator gleamed in the dark kitchen; an oilcloth-covered table stood on wide, pine floorboards with tin can lids nailed over the spaces where knots had fallen through. Pink frills curtained the one tiny window. Andorra glanced at the ceiling as she entered. Whole trunks of trees stripped of bark, *vigas,* were laid as beams with split pieces of cedar crosswise between them, the wood enriched by a patina of age and smoke. Thank goodness Adelina hadn't modernized by covering the beams with pressed board; except for the fancy refrigerator, Andorra's second home was unchanged. Adelina placed the half moons of ice respectfully into glasses, poured the Coke and joined Andorra at the table.

"Eee, Andorra. Someone is renting the old Duran place. I didn't think it would bother you. He pays me the rent in cash and I have it for you."

"No, Auntie. Better you should keep the money for yourself for all the trouble of guarding the house. I'm sorry I still don't know what to do with Papi's property. Who is renting it?"

"An artist. They say he goes to Europe to sell his paintings. Ellie told me they are paintings of rocks—she went up to see things—but he didn't have much to say. He's polite when he pays me the rent and always on time."

Andorra would pass the old Duran place on her way to La Escondida. "I'll see if he's there tomorrow. I'm content that someone is in the house. I know the old houses won't survive without care."

"When you're married you'll come and live here. I'll watch your children grow. But *¡hija!* I'm not going to live forever and I want to see you married. Look, your father and his sister are at their rest and their brother, Reuben, gone since so many years in the Bataan. Reuben, he was one for a laugh—like his father. You would have loved them." She sighed. "*Así es.*" Such is life.

"Oh, Auntie, don't be sad. Look, we are together after so long. And you will have many years. And I should count the minutes until you start talking about marriage. Don't worry. I'm young yet, don't you think?"

"Young! I had three children when I was your age and Hector was ten. I don't know why young people think they have so much time these days." Adelina saw Andorra's face cloud. "Don't let me bother you, *mijita*. I'm a foolish old woman. I know there is happiness for a girl so sweet."

It would be nothing less than cruel to tell Adelina she didn't want children and couldn't picture any man she'd want to marry. Andorra squeezed her hand and smiled.

Two

Still on England time, Andorra slept poorly and woke late. After more posole for breakfast, she filled a pack with the rosewood box, a canning jar of water, a sandwich, and a little spade that belonged to Adelina's great-grandson—there was no counting on Papi's tools still being there. She wore the boots, jeans and T-shirt she had packed for the hike. It would be an easy day, there and back, and the fall air held a delicious crispness beneath the sun's warmth. She promised to make tamales with Adelina that night.

The little rental car was soon out of Estancia and not long after that, off the paved road and into wilder country. The rugged terrain was draped with yellow and subtle green where erosion had not stripped away garments of sage, rabbitbrush and goldenrod, revealing the private ruddy colors of the earth. The road climbed past a house here and there, dipped to cross an arroyo and climbed again. There was the wide spot where you parked to get down to the waterfall, and just a bit beyond another arroyo and immediately after, the turnoff.

The car didn't have the clearance for the ruts carved in the clay, but Andorra skillfully danced it over their tops to protect the undercarriage and brought it successfully through to a wide parking area where she saw a large new pick-up, a plywood crate, and beyond them, the old Duran place. Even though the house had belonged to her father's family since he was a child, such names died hard here. The adobe house had a tin roof heavily stained with rust and a long portál—a flat-roofed porch—on one side.

As she parked the car, she was startled by the sight of a naked man bathing beside the hand pump in front of the house. Andorra stared as lather ran down his body, chased by water he poured from a bowl. His chest and shoulders were as broad as a swimmer's, his legs long and graceful and his sex of immodest size.

With eyes closed, he rinsed the soap from his hair; when he opened them he caught her staring. Andorra blushed and retreated into a busy inspection of the front seat.

Through her dark curls, she glanced again as the man turned away, wrapped a towel around his hips and splashed water on his feet. He walked calmly toward the house, stepped up to the porch and disappeared into shadow. Andorra was still in the car when he reemerged in jeans and a neatly tucked shirt. She stayed busy looking in the glove compartment and back seat until, as the man approached the car, there was nothing to do but get out and introduce herself.

"I am sorry to have come up on you like this. I'm Andorra Sandoval."

"Andorra?

"Yes."

"Like the country?"

"Yes. People don't usually know that. Though it's actually a principality."

"Not a country?"

"No. Bit of an anachronism."

"I'm Nicholson White. Nick. How do you do?" They shook hands.

"Very well, thank you," Andorra said, looking away. What could they do but try to pretend the meeting was only just beginning?

"Adelina is a Sandoval. Are you related to her?"

"She's my great-grandfather's brother's grandson's wife. Or rather widow." Andorra laughed nervously and wiped perspiration from her upper lip. "I think that's right. My father's some degree of cousin, by marriage. I call her my auntie. I was born here. Well, not *here* but up the arroyo a few miles. We used to live at La Escondida."

Nick stared down at her, tall as she was. "What is La Escondida?"

"It's an old name for the house. It means the Hidden Place."

"You don't sound like you're from here."

"Oh, I am, but I'm from England too. I live in London now. It always takes me a while to temper my accent. You see, the reason I'm here, the reason I've barged in here, is that... Well, I've come to bring my father's ashes up to the house. He died two years ago. I know it's a long time but I was finishing school..." Andorra could have kicked herself; she'd never sounded so daft. This man completely unnerved her and first sight had, in some sense, propelled them into intimacy. Oh, what rot. It had done no such thing. She had seen naked men before, for Christ's sake.

Nick noted her confusion, and her startling good looks. "I didn't know there was another house up there. Is there a way to drive?"

"No. I'll have to walk. We used to have horses to get in and out. Do you mind if I park here for the day?"

"Of course not. I don't want to keep you." That not being strictly true, he added, "Can I give you something to drink before you go?"

"Yes, that would be brilliant. The day's hotter than I thought. I have some water to take with me, but I wouldn't mind topping up."

"Come on in." Nick stepped back and swung an arm.

"I haven't been in this house in a long time," she said as she stepped onto the stones laid around the hand pump and up to the house, avoiding the mud where the water had run into the yard. As she climbed the two steps to the porch she saw a collection of bleached bones along the edge and thought of Georgia O'Keeffe. Cruel of her, she'd left so little for the painters who followed. Inside the door was the old kitchen. No new refrigerator here, or any refrigerator. A rickety chair sat at the handmade wooden table; the counters were made from barky 2x4s; four kerosene lamps, enough for reading, clustered beside a double bed with a blue and white, hand-woven coverlet. The room was conspicuously clean.

Andorra could see a painting through the door into the other room and she was immediately drawn to it. In colors looking as if they had been washed clean by a long rain, a rock of immense presence emerged from a shimmering blue sky with a bird hovering above—half Red-tailed Hawk, half atmospheric phenomenon.

"Pardon, may I look? That really is quite lovely."

"Nothing is really ready for viewing," Nick said, quietly closing the door. "I'm sorry. I feel uncomfortable showing my work before I've finished."

Andorra, like all beautiful people, was not accustomed to having doors closed in her face but she also hesitated to let anyone see her unfinished work. It didn't feel exactly rude, but not welcoming either.

"I'll get your water, or would you prefer coffee?"

"Do you have tea?"

"Sorry, no."

"Coffee is lovely, if it's no trouble."

"Not at all. Please have a seat."

I want to prolong this, Andorra realized as she watched the man preparing the coffee. His fingers were very long and his hands moved with conspicuous grace. Dark hair curling damply around his ears didn't look as though it had been cut recently and he had a day's growth of beard; he made it look like a fashion statement. The shirt, which showed more than a few paint smears, had once been fine and his jeans were close around his legs—designer cut, not jeans bought at the Farm Supply. On his feet were fine leather huaraches. Nicholson White. His name would not be forgotten.

While water boiled, he reached for the chair at the foot of the bed, easily swung it up to the table and placed two rustic cups on the scoured wood.

"Milk? I just went to town and can actually accommodate you."

"Yes, milk and sugar."

Nick bent to look under the counter and held up a small bag of sugar that dropped a fine stream from a hole in the corner.

"Mice. Do you mind?"

"No. I'm used to it. How did you come to find this place?"

"Gerard Paulson found it for me. The gallery owner in Santa Fe? I had a show there last year and I wanted to come back to the area to work; I like to do each show in a different part of the world. This work will be shown in Berlin." He nodded toward the closed door as he put a bowl containing the sugar and a milk carton on the table.

Andorra tried to keep herself from staring. His eyes were especially attractive, intelligent and healthy. White teeth too. "Where else have you worked?"

"The show I did for Gerard was painted in a village in the Pyrenees. I was in France for six months and before that I was in Greece for a while."

"You are very footloose," observed Andorra.

Nick poured the coffee without comment. I must have gone too far, she thought as they sipped in awkward silence. Glancing around the room, she noticed how awfully primitive the furnishings looked and wished they had been upgraded. The lack of running water was embarrassing, and there could be at least a gas refrigerator; she should purchase one before she left.

"Are you comfortable here?" she asked.

"I love it, actually, living without electricity. I think this will be the first group of paintings I've painted entirely in the daytime."

Conversation failed again. Finally, she pushed her chair back. "I've intruded long enough. Thank you for the coffee. I'll be on my way."

"I'm afraid I've been rude," Nick said abruptly. "I

seem to have forgotten my social graces." He gazed out the open door toward the mesa. "It's so silent. I'm sure there are hardly any places like this left in the world."

"No, there're not. I'm grateful for every moment I spend here. It's a cliché that you can hear yourself think, but you have to believe it was inspired by land like this." Her voice had lowered as though to honor the pristine quiet. Nick looked into Andorra's eyes for the first time. The intensity of his gaze drew her in and then, as though magnetic poles had switched, quickly made her avoid it.

"Hear yourself think? Sometimes the sound is deafening," he said with a short laugh. "No, forgive me. This place is magical. I've loved being here."

Andorra stood. "I must go." She saw the closed door again. "That painting. You caught the clarity of the light."

"Thank you. I tried." He nearly smiled.

Outside, Andorra fetched the pack containing the rosewood box from the car and shrugged it onto her back. The little shovel hung from the drawstring and swung as she moved quickly toward the arroyo. She turned, and seeing Nick watching her, raised a hand. He returned the gesture. She would have been pleased to know he had noticed her breasts straining against the T-shirt as she shouldered the pack and that he watched her hips until she disappeared up the trail.

At first, Andorra's thoughts stayed on Nick. The encounter had left her tense, excited. His body! She couldn't get the image out of her head. She found herself reviewing what had happened, including the embarrassing moments. He had in turn been distant, bitter, almost intimate. It occurred to her that he seemed very sad.

But with each step and familiar sight, his image retreated. She was drawn back into her past, her childhood: riding horseback over this very trail; finding the rattlesnake in the path; flushing jackrabbits. She once had weighed as little to her father as he now did to her. Tears pricked her eyes at the thought.

Beyond an empty corral, the path entered the arroyo—the one she had crossed on the road and followed up the rutted drive—and soon squeezed through an outcrop of granite, the trail narrowing and the sides rising above her head. Eventually, broad natural stairs let her climb out of the watercourse to follow from above for nearly a mile. The path diverged from the arroyo and entered a great bowl of ashy, blue-green sagebrush with boulders grandstanding on three sides. The perfume of the twisted bushes rose around her as she brushed past them on the overgrown trail. To one side she saw her special place—a rock that was easy to scale and large and smooth enough to lie back on and contemplate the sky until you seemed to merge into it. How many times would she be here again? The day was young; she could make a quick visit.

She detoured off the trail, slung her pack down by the base, took a sip of water from her canning jar, and crawled up the easy slope of the boulder. The top seemed smaller than when she had found it as a child but was still big enough for her long legs and outstretched arms. With her eyes closed tightly to the sun, she soaked up the warmth above and below her body.

She had called the man—Nick—footloose. And me, she thought? No mother or father, brothers, sisters or lovers. She had been wondering if it was right to hold on to her land and houses, as though part of her actually wished to cut her last tether. Did she want to return to London? Her school connections were there, but where did she really belong? Did she dare for her own sanity to sever the roots she had here in New Mexico? Part of her problem was the same one generations of young people had faced—making a life in such remoteness—but what was valuable if not a claim to a place on this earth, a vantage for watching friends and family move through the stages of their lives? Her life: what to do with it and where to do it? Again she thought of Nick. Strange for that brief encounter to seem so powerful...

Had she dozed off? Suddenly she was aware that the red she had seen through her eyelids had turned black. A breeze was drying the sweat on her body and bringing it close to chill. Andorra sat up and found the sun obscured by ominous purple clouds; without doubt it was going to rain. She leapt from the rock, grabbed her pack and trotted back across the meadow to the trail in its center. As she paused to get the pack onto her shoulders, she considered going back, but having come more than halfway, she continued on toward a space between the boulders where the trail twisted down around jumbled rocks and tree roots. As she descended, she remembered her sweet little mare, Sunbeam, picking her way delicately around the obstacles. She passed under the magnificent spruce that was another childhood treasure and came at last to the grassy place with sheer cliffs on the side she had come down and the arroyo, encountered again, on the other. Beyond it, equally abrupt cliffs rose to complete an embrace.

She was startled to see the arroyo running with

heavy, brown water; it must already be raining higher up. As Andorra watched, the level abruptly rose a foot, and a few seconds later another high surge rolled past and proceeded determinedly downstream. She realized she wouldn't make it to the house as the first drops of icy rain fell on her shoulders.

There was a cave at the base of the cliff farther into the meadow and she ran for it, sprinting at the end, the spade banging against her, as the world became all pelting water. She was soaked to the skin by the time she crawled into the shallow shelter. The rain made a dull gray curtain over the lip of the overhang and a rivulet ran inside and began to pool under her hips. Two packing boxes sat beside her, one on top of the other. Printing proclaimed that each contained two dozen boxes of Sudafed. What on earth were they doing here?

Andorra shivered miserably. If only she could have had water back at the house and that nice hot coffee now. Suddenly famished, she dug in the pack for the sandwich. As she chewed on Adelina's bread, bologna, tomato, and mayonnaise, nagging worries began. Storms over the mountains could make the arroyo run for hours. The beginning of the trail near the old Duran place couldn't be navigated when the narrow passage was filled with water; she might have to stay overnight at the house. Even worse, she suddenly recalled that Sudafed was an ingredient in homemade methamphetamine—crystal meth. Just before her last visit, a meth lab had been discovered in a trailer a few miles away when it caught fire; everyone had been talking about it. She felt a swift kick of fear and the bite of sandwich threatened to stick in her throat. She wrapped the rest as she fought for calm and wondered what she had gotten herself into.

After five or ten minutes, the rain tapered off and stopped. Andorra crawled out of the shelter and stood upright, water still dribbling from her hair, T-shirt plastered to her body, streaks of mud from the cave doing their best to cover her. The arroyo thundered. Standing beside it where the trail reached the meadow, contemplating the roiling water, was Nick.

Andorra felt a surge of relief. He had come after her.

Three

"Nick! Nick! Here!" she yelled over the roar of water pounding through the channel.

He swung around, quickly came up and took in her soaked hair and clothes. "Look at us!" He encompassed their wetness with arms wide. "I hope you don't mind my following you. When that storm came up—"

"You made it through the arroyo!"

"Only just. The water was rising fast when I found the trail leading out. Lucky I did."

"You could have been swept away."

"I nearly was."

"This is a mess. I was so foolish to assume the rainy season was over. I know better. But look, I've found something very scary—cases of Sudafed." Andorra brought him over to the cave. "You know what that's for—methamphetamine. I have a dreadful feeling somebody's using my father's house. We can't get down with the arroyo running, and the last thing we want to do is barge in on a meth lab!"

"Okay. Let's think. Here, I've got coffee." He put his pack on a rock and reached in for the thermos.

Andorra's laugh was interrupted by a shiver. "You have no idea how much I was wanting some of your coffee."

"How far are we from your father's house?" Nick asked as he poured into the lid and handed it to her. The coffee had milk and lots of sugar; nothing had ever tasted so good.

"Perhaps a quarter of a mile."

"Can we get close and see what's going on without being seen?"

"We should be able to."

"Maybe everything will be fine and we can go in and warm up. There must be a wood stove, right? Are there any other houses nearby that they might be using?" Andorra shook her head.

"Those boxes are pretty dirty. Maybe it's not happening now." He took a gulp of coffee and reassembled the thermos.

"We may as well go see," Andorra said as she slipped her pack over her shoulders. "This way." She moved off quickly and Nick followed up a path that squeezed between trees and tumbling water.

She couldn't remember having seen the arroyo run so fiercely. Chunks of earth on the sides were being undermined and washed in. Best not get too close; anyone falling in would never get out. She remembered the flood when little Sammy Griego had fallen into the Rio Oscuro by his house in Estancia and his body had been found against an irrigation dam in the Rio Grande fifty miles downstream.

When the trail crossed rocks slippery from the rain, Nick grasped Andorra's elbow and steadied her. His touch was the only warmth in a damp and chilly world where trees shook like wet dogs and bushes wiped themselves dry as they passed. Andorra's teeth chattered. Muscles clenched with cold were awkward as they climbed and slipped and teetered against each other.

The trail left the arroyo and eventually reached a place where pines stepped back to make an open space filled with sunflowers. The land rose gently toward a cluster of buildings: a barn, sheds and a long house with a tin-roofed porch; behind them it climbed more steeply and the pines gave way to aspens. The buildings appeared deserted, although the tall flowers largely obscured the view.

At that moment the world blazed red-orange, as though a theater director had cried, "Cue lights!" The sunflowers and autumn-yellow aspens seemed to ignite as the sun made a grand appearance beneath the layer of cloud that had brought the storm. The air was thick with color, saturated with the hue of gold brought to the melting point.

"Look at this," Andorra said, her voice full of awe. "It happens all the time after a rain. There's always a rainbow too. Look! You can just see the end. Oh, there it goes!" She pointed at its high arch. "It's a double! Have you ever seen such beauty?"

"No, the truth is, I haven't. I've watched this happen all summer. I tried to paint it but—"

The slam of a screen door interrupted him. Nick pulled Andorra into a crouch and they retreated into the shadow of the pines.

"Bad luck," he whispered as they squatted behind a tree. Nick pressed his knuckle against his lips; a plan was needed, and quickly, with the approach of night and the arroyo unrelenting. "Is there a hut or barn or any shelter that can't be seen from the house?"

"There is. The old mine. It's just back there and over the ridge. We could make a fire and no one would know," Andorra whispered. "Come on. I'll show you."

Bending low, she crept back through the trees, up an incline, and around an outcrop of jutting rock. Again they could hear the roaring water. "Here it is," she said as Nick came up behind her; she gestured to what appeared to be no more than sloping forest floor. Dark, dried leaves and needles were spattered with coins of aspen leaf that had made their way past the canopy. Andorra slid down through the litter, turned and ducked out of sight. Nick followed. Under a low roof of partially rotted boards, a space nearly eight feet wide ended at an earthfall fifteen feet in. Pieces of wood, some that had apparently once been wall supports, were strewn about among the dead leaves that covered the floor.

"Very cozy. We can burn this wood?" Nick asked.

"Wait. I don't have any matches!"

"I do."

"Oh my God, you're a lifesaver!" Andorra watched with grateful respect as Nick pulled a plastic-wrapped box of kitchen matches from his pack, knelt and began clearing a space for the fire.

She kicked at some wood among the leaves. "This must be the old goat-milking stanchion. It will burn nicely," she said as she squatted and began pulling the nailed bits apart. A pile of fence posts near the opening proved to be rotting, but dry, and she dragged them over beside Nick. Outside the molten gold had cooled and slag gray was advancing through the trees.

Nick had found twigs and piled them with dried leaves in between. He built his fire as he had made his coffee, Andorra observed, slowly, enjoying the process. They were silent, focused on the smoke that began to curl and rise as the leaf kindling caught, then on the flame that danced among the twigs, and finally on the exuberant flare of the larger pieces she had provided— all the warmth, protection and elemental fascination of the hearth.

It soon became apparent, however, that the mine would fill with smoke.

"We're going to be driven out. I'd better try to make a chimney," Nick said. He chose one of the posts, jammed it between two of the overhead boards and twisted. The boards parted with a shower of rotted wood and composted leaves that came down on top of the fire, threatening to extinguish it.

"That was clever," Nick said sarcastically as

36

Andorra gave a yelp, but the fire forgave him and immediately sprang up again. He worked the post more carefully until the hole was enlarged and smoke reached for the passage in the roof.

"I'm not much of a mountain man." He sat back from the fire, smiling.

"You must be joking. You're doing brilliantly." She was feeling nearly giddy with relief at the companionship and the fire's warmth.

While Andorra added several pieces of wood to the flames, Nick looked around their little hiding place. "Let's make a stand for hanging our clothes. We have to get dry. How about our pack strings for a clothesline?" he suggested.

They each extracted their strings; tied together, the cords extended nearly five feet. A nail in a part of the mine's wall still braced with wood anchored one end while Nick wedged the other into a split in a fence post that he jammed at an angle between the dirt floor and the roof boards.

"I'm afraid, me proud beauty, you're going to have to take off those jeans."

He was right; her clothes were miserably wet. The joke eased the awkwardness and made Andorra laugh, but reminded her of the beautiful body she had seen earlier.

They removed shoes and socks and propped them near the fire. Nick worked his damp jeans over his hips revealing maroon briefs and those long legs. Trying not to look at him, Andorra tugged her jeans at the hip, the leg, the hip again, eventually handing them over. While Nick draped them as near the fire as he dared, she hid behind bent knees and crossed ankles.

"What do you think, Andorra?" She glanced quickly at him as he spoke. He had remembered her name too. Though they were alone and half naked, it was her name on his lips that brought home the intimacy.

"Wonderful," she said, and meant it.

"How did you get named for a 'principality'?" He grinned at her as he unbuttoned his shirt, pulled it off and put it on the line.

"I think my mother just liked the sound. She took me there once. I remember she used her French and I used my Spanish. People didn't know what to make of us, I'm sure. I've heard it's one big duty-free these days."

"You speak Spanish."

"The local Spanish, yes."

"Is it very different?"

"There are unique idioms, some words are

38

different from Castilian, at least modern Castilian; we like to think it's archaic, closer to sixteenth-century Spanish, but I'm not sure—I'm not a linguist—and you can get along with it anywhere in my experience."

"Sixteenth-century Spanish?"

"This area was settled then. Conquistadors, armor, pikes...all that."

"Interesting. You'd better get your shirt off too," Nick said as he casually looked toward the smoke hole.

Andorra slipped off her T-shirt and leaned modestly toward her bent legs as Nick hung it on the cords. In a moment she got on her knees and shook out her hair, ran her fingers through the thick, dark mass and pulled at the tangles until the curls reluctantly separated. Nick took the opportunity to gaze at her body; his quickly began to respond. He reached for his pack and put it across his lap as she tossed her hair and sat back.

"Look at this. I grabbed some cheese and apple pie. They're from the farmers' market and the pie was, in fact, made by Adelina."

"She made one for us too! I can't believe it—we're going to feast. I have most of a sandwich here," she said as she pulled her pack near. "Well, about a half." She made a face at the pitiful lump. "I suppose we should save the pie for dessert. Here's your sandwich entrée."

"Hmm, bologna. Classy."

"Auntie's other specialty."

They ate ravenously, devouring every crumb and drinking all Andorra's water. Tomorrow would have to take care of itself. At least there'd be a swallow of coffee from the thermos. When the food was gone, the clothes checked (nearly dry, at least the shirts) and the fire built up again, Andorra offered an assessment.

"I think we should get out of here first thing in the morning. The arroyo will be dry, I'm sure. I'll get the sheriff to check out the house. If there's a meth lab over there I don't think we should fool with it. Those people can be fierce about protecting their investment. What do we have—a child's shovel—to defend ourselves?"

"You're probably right. Why don't we try to get closer tomorrow to see if that's really what's going on? Maybe we're over-reacting and we've got a runaway teen that can just be told to go home. Maybe you could still bury your father's ashes."

"Oh, dear. Papi's ashes. This is pretty far from the little ceremony I wanted. And Adelina is going to be so worried. I wish we could get back tonight. But listen. You can still hear the arroyo running." They easily made out its deep whoosh and beneath that the clacking of boulders tumbled by the current. It sounded ferocious.

"Do you think she'll send searchers out tonight?"

"If she did, they'd find they couldn't get up here, but people are sure to come tomorrow. I hope she thinks I'm snug in the house. Perhaps she won't worry too much."

Nick had felt her T-shirt several times and eventually took it off the line. He worked the fabric to see if some of the mud would come off but little did.

"Here. This feels nice and warm."

Andorra pulled the shirt over her head. "Oooh, wonderful. Try yours. Talk about simple pleasures." She hugged herself and squirmed, catching Nick's full attention. He thought her sensuous wiggle was pretty unfair. Her closeness and frivolous underwear were nearly more than he could stand so tempted was he to reach out a hand to that firm arm and pull her to him. No permission asked, no clever words—if he could think of any—just pull her over until his lips reached hers.

Nick quelled the fantasy as best he could. Not appropriate, not now. He'd help her out of this fix but that was all. That was all. He put on his own dry shirt.

"Nick, this is really wonderful. Your pie and coffee and matches! I feel as though I never learned a thing growing up here. Of course, I mostly grew up elsewhere, if that doesn't sound like a pitiful excuse."

"Where? In London?"

"Some, but also Europe—Spain, Italy. Trips everywhere."

"How was it you left here?"

"My mother took me away. She was from England." Andorra didn't see Nick's frown as she stared into the flames. "Going off with her and leaving my father nearly killed me," she said softly. Nick threw a piece of wood on the fire and sparks flew. Startled, Andorra looked up, but didn't notice that his mood had changed.

"My mother was not really interested in me. I don't know why she didn't let me stay where I was happy—Papi and I were very close. Her life was parties, holidays, the 'rich and famous.' Sometimes I was with her; sometimes I was left with people I hardly knew; but I was under her spell for a long time. She was amazing—so beautiful, so clever—but absolutely not the mothering type. Oh, dear, I'm sorry. I'm sounding pitiful again. I survived."

"Is your mother still in England?"

"No, she's gone. She was killed in a car accident just after I brought my father to live with me in London. Near where Princess Grace died in Monaco—I know she would have loved the parallel. Who knows? It's possible she even chose it; she had such a terror of growing old. I'm sure she wouldn't have come to see us anyway. She always resented her time with him. He'd had a stroke and couldn't live on his own and, finally, he died. I loved taking care of him even though it was a challenge while I was in school. You know, I wasn't sad when my mother died. That sounds horrible, doesn't it. I couldn't stop trying to please her when she was alive but when she was gone I felt more relief than anything else, that and a good dose of self-pity. She always disapproved of me. I don't think she taught me anything except that I don't want children. That's not fair—she taught me how much to tip the concierge when times were good and how to skip out on the bill when they weren't. But I felt so alone when I lost my father. I think I've hardly been living for the last two years and here I am ready to say goodbye and let him go—and now this." Then Andorra brightened and made a flip with her hand. "Papi would have enjoyed it though. He always liked to be in the middle of things. I should throw his ashes into that meth fiend's eyes, tie him up, and march him out at shovel point. That would be the sort of thing Papi'd like."

Nick laughed in spite of the story's sting and turned away to check the jeans. The waistbands were still damp though at least the moisture was warm. Even now they would feel good and they certainly couldn't lie on these prickly leaves without them. But he would be lying, he thought with bleak emotion, near this girl who was pushing every painful button. What good was it to scatter his days around the globe if a chance encounter in some remote place could result in this?

"When are you going back?" he asked after a time.

"To the UK? In about three weeks. Where is your home?"

"I'm footloose. Remember?"

Andorra glanced at him to see if he was as cross as that abrupt answer suggested. Nick heard himself. "I'm sorry. I really haven't had more than a storage unit for a few years now. Before that I lived in New York. I was born in Chicago."

"No family?"

"Parents, cousins. I was married. Things didn't work out. I don't mean to be rude. I hate to talk about it."

Andorra searched for a topic. "Well then, tell me about your art."

"Okay. I guess I can be civil about that. I'm better at painting than I was at being married, although I'm not as good as I'd like to be. I say that I work at the interface between realism and abstraction. I take the most material of matter—rocks—and try to show the space within the atomic particles, to render them insubstantial and at the same time dense enough to bend light, both celebrating gravity and defying it—gravity in various uses: the seriousness of reality, the absurdity of it; the weight of existence and something like 'the incredible lightness of being.' Does that make any sense?"

Andorra laughed. "Let's see. I may have to think about it, but it certainly was an impressive, umm, can I say spiel without being insulting?"

"I don't think you can say it without being all too perceptive." Nick smiled. "You learn to talk like that in New York. Please don't question me too closely on what it all means. You, or at least your agent or gallery owner, have to be some kind of rap artist or poet or philosopher. You intimidate clients: Are you sufficiently post-modern to own this work?"

"What *is* post-modernism?"

"Whatever, it's not as relevant as whether you have enough money to buy the painting."

"Don't be so cynical. I got that glimpse. Your work is exquisite. It doesn't require knowledge of the laws of physics either."

"Thanks. It may also be that I just like to work with my hands."

"I can see that. You made a very graceful cup of coffee."

"I did?"

"Yes. That's interesting about our true motivations for what we do—what you said about working with your hands. Sometimes I think I chose the fifteenth and sixteenth centuries to study because the old reference materials are such a sensual delight."

"So you're a historian instead of a linguist. Do you teach?"

"I might some day. At the moment I want to write a book. But tell me, why aren't you in New York busy making clients insecure?"

"Yeah, well. As you see, I've started hiding out. I think I told you I painted in France last year and the year before I was on a tiny Greek island. Not a tourist in sight. Old women dressed in black, if you can believe that's still going on. I've gotten a lead on a place to stay in Scotland after my December show. I have some ideas for paintings of waves crashing onto rocks, or through rocks—I'm still fascinated by rocks. New Mexico has been wonderful. Great rocks." Nick smiled into Andorra's attentive eyes. Her newly dried hair was wild and her face was smooth, glowing and calm in the flickering light. He found himself wanting to tell her his story.

"Don't you like to hang out with other artists? Drink into the small hours? Collect groupies?" she teased.

"You sound like you've known some artists. Yeah, I've tried all that. I guess that's how I got my wife. That was in New York. It wasn't a good scene—booze, cocaine, heroin. I hope I don't shock you. I had a very close friend who overdosed. He really had talent too. A sweet guy. You were either dulling the pain because you were so exquisitely sensitive to life or getting consciousness out of the way so you could plumb your depths. I'm afraid my ex-wife is well on her way to China by now."

"Why are you afraid? Do you still care for her?" Andorra found herself very much wanting to know.

"I care for her less than I can say. She did a terrible thing." He poked at the coals with the end of a post before putting it on them. The wood flared. "It's not unlike your story, Andorra, too much like it, in fact. She took my daughter away and I don't know where she is."

"I'm *so* sorry. That must have been awful listening to what I said. I can imagine how hard this is for you, and your daughter. You were close?"

"Yes."

"How old is she?"

"She's thirteen now."

"How long since you've seen her?"

"Since she was eleven. I've been trying to track her over two years. I've hired someone to help but so far all I've gotten are dead ends. Actually, I'm flying to New Orleans in a couple of days. My detective thinks she's there."

"I hope it works out. Then you'll come back?"

"Yes. I've almost got the paintings done. I'll come back to finish and pack." Nick paused and added fiercely, "She's all I can think about. I worry more about her every day. I hate that she must think I've abandoned her. I've kept the number in New York with a message service but she's never called." He put another piece of wood on the fire and stared into it. "Look," he sighed, "we'd better try to get some sleep. I think these jeans are ready." He felt them again. "Yeah, they'll do."

Andorra struggled into her warm jeans, took the box from her pack, and rolled the nylon up for a pillow. When Nick was dressed, he put his pack a little distance farther into the mine and they lay down with the fire between them and the entrance.

"Are you comfortable?" Nick asked.

"Not bad. Oh, I'm on a rock." She reached under her hip and then dusted her hands. "Can you feel the heat?"

"It's good," he mumbled, smiling at her unwitting double meaning.

But Andorra could feel the heat too—the fire's on one side and his on the other. She began to imagine what would happen if she turned to him or inched her hips closer. I'm too excited to go to sleep, she thought, and then she was gone, exhausted from jet lag, cold, anxiety, and a day of high emotion and painful memory.

Nick did not fall asleep so easily. His own arousal and memory were too strong. He, too, imagined bridging the distance between their bodies; imagined how easily the jeans might come off a second time; imagined seeing again those barely covered hips, those long, lovely legs. He also saw the complications of such an encounter, the impossibility of merging another life with his own, obsessed as he was with his loss. His mind drifted momentarily to the possibility of new love, even new children, but how could he risk it? Deborah had been so beautiful and alive; he'd only realized how flawed and crazy when it was too late. I can't tell about a woman, Nick thought, but this one…what a beauty. It had been a long time. Sleep came at last.

Sleep came but his desire continued in his dreams. Andorra woke later to find their bodies tightly spooned and the pressure of an erection against her. Was he awake? She stopped her breathing to hear his. He seemed to be asleep; he was very still. Both frustration and desire mounted. If only there was a way to join their bodies, and not deal with it in the morning.

While she lay awake, a breeze slipped past the dying fire to bring the smell of moisture, pine and the earth of home. The house with its warm memories was so near. She remembered her father sitting beside her after dinner, working patiently through history and algebra, showing her how to improve a paragraph or reciting her spelling words, always making it fun. "If an urchin steals an apple at three o'clock and runs away at ten feet per second and a policeman sees him at one minute after three—" An *urchin.* She remembered how funny she'd thought that was.

Her father's own education had stopped after one year at the University of New Mexico, but his mind had been sharp and his interests broad. The house had been without television or radio—so quiet—but books, newspapers and magazines had been piled about. He always had textbooks waiting for her when she came for the summer; Aunt Lydia had made sure a complete set passed from the school where she taught to her brother's hands. He'd been the best kind of teacher, always telling her how smart she was, and she'd found herself prepared for her next grade level and more when she returned to her mother. In that life, school was sometimes a fine establishment for English expats, when the money was flowing; sometimes a place where she blundered in a foreign language. For a while, a tutor traveled with them but when he actually started showing interest in his teaching duties, he'd mysteriously disappeared.

And Papi had made sure she spoke Spanish. Everyone here was bilingual, except the hippies. Speaking it was one thing she could do better than her mother. She'd aced the university's foreign language requirement with a perfect score. Dear Papi. She slept.

The next time she woke it was to the unwelcome sight of a man and a dog silhouetted in the dim early light at the mine entrance.

Four

Andorra sprang fully awake and sat up. Nick stirred beside her.

"I'll be damned. It's Andy!" the man said, squatting at the opening and steadying himself with a shotgun. "I didn't expect to see you up here. I thought you were far away somewhere."

"Lloyd? Lloyd? Is that you?" Andorra said with alarm. Lloyd had been the town bad boy from as far back as she could remember: fights at school; stealing firewood, tools, jewelry, video recorders—which had more than once resulted in jail time. He wasn't very good at not getting caught. "What are you doing up here?"

"Well, let's see. Lookit that! You've got a friend with you. Guess I'm havin' visitors. Let's have you outta there. You haven't got a gun have you? Okay, easy. Come on."

There was nothing to do but crawl out into the open. Lloyd Leyba was scrawny and his eyes were dim and red-rimmed. He looked like a Hollywood maniac, only worse—real. He danced back out of any reach, grinning and exulting.

"Looky here. I've got Andy. Andy's come to visit. Oooh, baby. Am I happy to see you. Oh, yeah. I know you too," he said, eyeing Nick. "You're down at the old Duran place. We been dodgin' you all summer. Good boy." He nudged the dog with his boot. "You done good this time." The dog simultaneously cringed and looked up adoringly.

"Lloyd," Andorra said, "what's going on? Are you at my father's place?"

"Mebbe I am. Mebbe you should go over there with me."

Andorra spoke firmly. "Look, Lloyd. Don't get yourself in trouble ordering us around with that gun. We'll just get out of here and you can think over whether you want to trespass. I don't want any trouble from you and I don't want to cause you any, but Adelina is expecting me and it's going to be better for everyone if I go back down now. If anyone comes up to check, you'll have had plenty of time to be somewhere else."

"I never did forget you, Andy. No way. I can see how sweet you looked when we'd swim in the river. All us boys had to stay under water, you gave us boners so bad. I could get one now just thinking about it." He giggled until Andorra's steely gaze sobered him.

"Wait a minute, Lloyd." Nick spoke casually. "We've got a thermos of coffee. I sure would like some. You too? Mind if I get it?" Not waiting for an answer, he bent over, entered the mine and picked up the thermos. Showing Lloyd that his other hand was empty, he made his way back to Andorra's side.

Lloyd looked tense and began to raise the shotgun toward Nick.

"Lloyd," Andorra said sharply, calling his attention to her, "how's your mother? Does she still have her goats? Is she still making that great goat cheese?"

"Yeah, she makes it," Lloyd said slowly, looking back and forth between Andorra and Nick.

Nick poured coffee into the lid of the thermos and offered it to Andorra. She could only pretend to drink and handed it back. He poured more as though he hadn't a care in the world.

"That's enough of—"

Lloyd's words were cut off with a yelp. With impressive speed, Nick had hurled the liquid into his face, dropped the thermos, and driven a fist into Lloyd's jaw. He toppled like a board into the leaves and Nick grabbed his shotgun. Andorra, wide-eyed, shook her head and gave a short laugh.

"My God, that was impressive. Is he dead?"

"I think my hand is. We'd better get out of here." Nick grabbed Andorra's wrist and they started up the slope. As they neared the crest of the hill, Andorra slipped on the leaves and went down on one knee, and when Nick turned back to pull her to her feet, he saw that Lloyd was sitting up, though looking too dazed to cause any trouble. They'd be over the hill and out of the meadow before he came to his senses, and the shotgun was with them. But why was Andorra looking so startled, staring up the hill with eyes wide and mouth open? He wheeled. Another man stood at the top; another shotgun pointed directly at them.

"Drop the shotgun, man. Drop it rat now."

Nick did as he was told.

"Hands up. Let's see those hands."

Nick and Andorra slowly raised their hands.

"Lloyd, you okay?"

Lloyd moaned, cursed and shoved away the dog, which was trying to help by licking his face. "Sheeit. I think I got a loose tooth," he whined piteously.

Andorra turned to look at him.

"Hey, girl. You can stand still," the man with the gun barked. He looked even scarier than Lloyd and in much better physical shape. Strangely, he had a full head of white hair, though he couldn't have been out of his thirties. Crude blue patterns covered his arms, hands and neck—prison tattoos.

"What's the matter with you idiots?" Nick asked angrily. "You're threatening us? With people from the village coming up here to find out where we are? You don't know who this is?" he asked the white-haired man. "This is Andorra Sandoval. She *owns* this place. Estancia is packed to the rafters with her relatives, all of whom are wondering why she didn't come home last night. How long before they make it up here, do you think? An hour? Ten minutes? *Thirty seconds?* You have a chance to be saving yourselves, running like hell. You've got a meth lab, right? That's not going to be bad enough for you? You want to make it worse?"

Andorra tried to control her panic. Maybe he shouldn't have said anything about a meth lab.

"Shut up, you fag." The gunman sounded unintimidated, but his little eyes were darting back and forth as though Nick had made some impression.

"Hey, Lloyd, get up. Get up here," the man shouted down the hill. Lloyd got to his feet slowly and began a stumbling climb.

"That guy sucker punched me, Vince," he complained.

"Aw, Lloyd," Nick groaned, "a guy with a gun is no sucker. He's fair game. Andorra, do you know this other loser?"

"No, no, I never saw him before," Andorra said in a breathless whisper.

"So he's someone Lloyd convinced to come to this safe spot, this hidden spot? Now we come up here and don't make it down when we're supposed to? What a couple of fools," Nick said, shaking his head in disgust.

"Lloyd, what the fuck? You said nobody ever came to this place."

"How was I to know she would show up? The old man's dead. How was I to know? Whaddaya wanna do, Vince? Maybe we should get outta here."

"They know who we are, asshole! They sure as hell know who you are!"

"Whaddya mean, Vince? You wanna shoot 'em?"

"Will you fucking stop using my name! I oughta shoot you!"

"Lloyd, listen to me," Andorra said, talking over her shoulder. "You remember how my father helped you? He always believed in you. You don't want to let him down by doing something to me and my friend, do you? I'll help you get out of this. I'll do everything I can. I promise."

"She's lyin', Lloyd. Don't be a idiot. She'll have us locked up forever if we let her go."

"Naw wait, Vince. We gotta think this thing through."

"Think something through with you? Don't make me laugh. That'll take way more time than we got."

Lloyd continued up the hill, giving Nick and Andorra a wide berth. He stopped and held his palms up.

"Listen, man, I got it. We can use them like, you know, human sheets, so we can get outta here in case anybody comes up. We'll take them down to the old Duran place an', an', an' take his truck! An' if we see any searchers, we can say we'll shoot if they don't let us go."

"It's human *shields*, idiot. An' then we got not just these two but who knows who else identifyin' us?"

59

"Oh, yeah. I see what you mean." Lloyd frowned.

Vince rolled his eyes but didn't look like he had a plan either.

"Okay," he said finally. "Let's tie them up while we figure this out. We'll put 'em in the barn. You guys first." He swung the barrel of the shotgun. "Up the hill. Get that shotgun, Lloyd." Vince stepped well to one side so Nick and Andorra could go ahead of him.

The sun was only now cresting the eastern ridge and slanting obliquely into the valley, backlighting the grasses and sunflowers and sparkling on a light frost that soon wet their shoes and pant legs. Andorra shivered.

"What are we going to do, Nick?" she whispered as they crossed the meadow toward the barn.

"I don't think we have to worry. I think these guys are going to run away and leave us behind," he said under his breath, trying to convey a reassurance he didn't feel. "See if you can think of some place we can run to if we get away. We'll just hope they self-destruct in the meantime. Listen to them." Lloyd and Vince were well behind but they could hear murmurs from Lloyd and an occasional "Shut up, will ya?" or "How stupid can you get?" from Vince. They didn't sound like the best of friends.

As Nick and Andorra passed into the barn, they were half blinded by the contrast between darkness and mote-filled slices of sunlight passing between the boards forming the east wall. A horse snorted and clunked a hoof against wood. As their eyes slowly adjusted, Vince and Lloyd came in behind them.

"Tie them up, Lloyd. I'll keep 'em covered," Vince said.

"I guess I can tie them to the stall here. You first." Lloyd gestured to Nick with a jerk of his chin. "Sit down there." He pointed to the base of the corner post. The horse shied to the far side of the stall as Nick lowered himself to the ground. Lloyd took one of two ropes coiled on top of the post and began threading it through the slats of the stall and around Nick's elbows and torso.

"That won't work, idiot," Vince said disgustedly. "He'll just get out of that."

"Listen here, Vince. I know what I'm doin' with ropes. Get over here, Andy."

Andorra hesitated. Vince shouted, "Move!" and she quickly placed herself beside Nick with her back to the post. While Lloyd pulled her tight against it with the second rope, Andorra quietly inhaled to expand her chest like a tricky horse planning to make its saddle slide off, but he sensed it and punched her sharply in the ribs.

She groaned, lost the air and bent over in pain.

"What the fuck?" Nick yelled. Lloyd immediately struck him hard across the mouth. Vince laughed.

"Shut up! You just shut up! You got more than that comin' to you," Lloyd shouted at Nick. He quickly finished his tying. Blood seeped into Nick's mouth. He managed to lean his head far enough over to spit into the dirt; a trickle of blood ran down his chin. Andorra felt panic rise at the sight, not daring to speak.

"Okay, Lloyd. Come on. We got work to do. Don't leave your shotgun." Vince turned on his heel and headed to the house. From the porch, he surveyed the meadow. No one. Were these searchers a bluff? Lloyd climbed the steps after him and they went inside, slamming the screen behind them.

"Are you okay?" Nick asked Andorra.

"Yes. And you?"

"It's all right. Look, we have to get free. Let's try getting this post out of the ground. What do you think, can we throw our weight back and forth? Come on, this way...back..." They soon found their rhythm and rocked the post further and further until with a crunch it broke off underground.

"Ha! Rotten!" Nick exulted, while Andorra quashed a moment's shame at the decrepitude of Papi's barn. "Let's see if we can get it out."

After a struggle, they got their legs under their bodies so they could lift the post. The jagged end came loose from the ground, making the cross pieces of the stall angle on their nails; one gave way entirely and sagged toward the dusty earth. Kneeling, they worked again to twist apart the disintegrating stall. More and more agitated, the horse turned in circles as the slats came loose; Andorra called to her softly. Finally, the rail between their ropes and the bottom of the post fell away.

Nick said, "Okay. Now you slide your rope off the end—"

"No! That never was the fuckin' deal!" Lloyd shouted from the house. Nick and Andorra exchanged anxious glances.

"Quick. I'll pull up, you pull down. Wiggle the ropes," Nick said urgently. Andorra gritted her teeth and twisted the cords, trying to make some slack. Using the opposite of her original tactic, she expelled all her air as she walked her ropes down the post. She gained a couple of inches; there still was a foot to go. She stretched the ropes again and again until they bit painfully into her arms. Three inches down…six…ten. She was free! Muffled shouting came from the house as she slipped from the ropes. The screen door slammed again. There was a deafening blast from a shotgun.

"Right! Run you little pussy!" they heard Vince yell. A jolting second explosion. Tingling silence.

Andorra frantically tackled Nick's ropes, digging in her fingernails and pulling. The ropes moved along the post until they wedged under a large splinter. She looked around and saw a broken shovel handle, grabbed the wood and used the metal grip to chop madly at the raised sliver and the rotting post, shearing off the edge. The ropes slipped down and Nick was free.

"Shhh," he said. They froze and listened for sounds from the house. Nothing. The mare stepped carefully over the collapsed edge of the stall, ambled up to Andorra and nuzzled her.

"It sounds like Lloyd might have split. Maybe Vince has too. We'd better be sure before we go out," Nick whispered, looking around the barn and up to the loft. "I'm going to get up there over the door. I can jump anybody who might come. You hide in back, okay?" They listened again. Still nothing. "Go on. Maybe no one will come."

Andorra went to the far end of the barn where remnants of straw bales made a wall behind which she could crouch unseen. She saw bits of hay filtering through the air as Nick positioned himself at the edge of the loft above the door. The horse followed her and poked her nose into the bedding straw; she had to be very hungry to be interested in the dry pile that must have been there since her father had stacked it.

Andorra didn't hear the footsteps over the sound of the horse's snuffling. Suddenly there was a shout, a thud, a scream of rage. Jumping up and peering around the horse, Andorra saw Nick grabbing Vince by the shoulders and throwing him into the barn wall. Vince got up slowly enough to give Nick time to get his hands on a slat and when Vince ran toward him, Nick swung awkwardly, clipping his shoulder. Vince lost his balance, rolled over toward a trough and struck his head. Again, he began to get to his feet. Unable to stay still any longer, Andorra shoved at the mare's rump and started around her.

A solid blast of sound stopped her dead. The horse reared and knocked her to the ground; it was all she could do to scramble away from its hooves. Then the screams began.

Five

The air was so thick with dust that for a long moment Andorra didn't know who had shot whom. Then she saw that Nick was the one standing and that it was Vince who was screaming as though all the devils in hell had come to drag him away. Andorra made her way past the horse and saw Vince rolling about on his back and holding his leg in the air, as blood welled from his boot.

"Jesus," Nick said. "I just wanted him to know I was serious."

Andorra looked at him and smiled a tremulous smile; at once, her legs wouldn't hold her up. With frequent glances toward Vince, Nick crouched beside her. He put his hand on her back and said gently, "Come on. Come on. It's all right. We're all right."

"Sorry. I'll be fine. I can't believe this."

Nick patted her while Vince's screams sagged into moans.

"Andooora, Andoooora." A cry came over the meadow. Suddenly re-energized, she jumped up and ran from the barn. The calls came again.

"I'm here!" she shouted as three men appeared among the sunflowers. "Jimmy! Armando! Elias!" She ran to meet them; she threw herself into Elias's arms, then hugged Armando and Jimmy.

"What's happened, *mijita*? What's happened? Thank goodness you're all right. Was that a shot?" Elias asked anxiously, just as Nick, holding the shotgun, emerged from the barn. With his bloody chin and limp, he looked as though he might well be the problem and the three men immediately went on guard. Feeling Elias stiffen, Andorra looked up to see Nick.

"It's all right. This is Nick White. Do you all know each other? He's been renting the old Duran place. Oh my God, how to tell you? Nick, these are my dear friends—Elias, Armando and Jimmy Medina."

Andorra took her head in her hands. "Lloyd

Leyba and another man, in the barn there, they… I came up yesterday to bury Papi's ashes. Oh, God. Papi's ashes." She squeezed her eyes shut. Seeing that she couldn't continue the story, Nick took it up.

"I saw her headed up here, and when the storm came in, I followed her," he said. "The guys were in the house and there were boxes of Sudafed around so we figured there must be a meth lab. The arroyo was so full we had to spend the night in the mine and Lloyd found us in the morning. He and this other guy, Vince, tied us up in the barn. Lloyd's either run off or he's dead out there. We got loose and then Vince and I fought and I took away his shotgun. I don't think he's going anywhere but I better get back to make sure." Nick couldn't suppress a grin and left the men exchanging looks in stunned silence. A moment later they followed him into the barn where Vince glared into their surprised faces. The horse snorted and tossed her head.

"What are we going to do with him?" Jimmy asked.

Armando shook his head. "I guess we have to haul him out of here. Jimmy, go see if Lloyd's lying out there somewhere. We better see to Andorra too." The three generations of Medina men left the barn.

Elias, an old friend of Aaron's, was in his

69

seventies, still handsome and vigorous. His eyes were edged with the deep grooves that come with frequent smiles. It had been he who sold the horses and cows and found homes for the dogs when Andorra took Aaron to London. Armando was his son and Jimmy his grandson. Armando was postmaster, head of the association of the *acequias*—irrigation ditches—and the husband of Elvira, Aaron's niece and the school principal. Jimmy had been the smallest of the gang that ran around together in summers past—the gang that included Andorra and sometimes, Lloyd.

Elias and Armando found Andorra standing in the meadow gazing toward the house. She smiled weakly when Elias wrapped his arm around her shoulder. Leaning against him, she listened to the wind in the pines and aspens behind the house. Golden leaves danced high in the air and descended around them. "Goldengrove unleaving," she thought as she reached up to catch one of the little fans, gazed at its perfect yellowness and slipped it into her pocket. The shushing trees commanded the stillness that had always been the soundtrack of summers at La Escondida, but, as if to remind her of the shattered peace, the sharp, cold smell of solvents thrust forward on the breeze.

"We'd better go see," Andorra said at last.

70

Piles of white plastic gallon containers lay on the ground around the steps, heaps of junk littered the porch and a shotgun leaned beside the door. Armando leapt forward, grabbed the gun and, ordering Elias and Andorra to wait, cautiously entered the house. In a moment he came back to the door.

"No one there. You're not going to like what you see," he said, shaking his head.

The kitchen was filthy: dishes, rags, plastic containers and piles of soft drink bottles were everywhere; ripped open Sudafed packages littered the floor and counters; tubing draped the *vigas* like artificial spider web in a Halloween haunted house, and all overlaid with a smell so overpowering they could hardly breathe. The once-beautiful blue-enameled cook stove, the large pot on it, the wall behind, and the ceiling above were covered with soot.

It took several moments before Andorra's eye found the traces of her life beneath the garbage. She realized the dirty dishes were the simple terra cotta she and Papi had found one summer on a trip over the Mexican border to Juarez. On the windowsill was the pitcher she liked to keep filled with flowers. This time of year it would have been bunches of aspen leaves; now a pair of pliers took their place. High on the wall was the picture of her father's parents, Ephraim and Maria. Her grandfather wore a dignified suit and a large moustache, and her grandmother peered through glasses with fins on the frames. Andorra knew them only from this photo in which Grandfather looked like Papi in bandito costume. The picture hung askew; she made her way across the room and reached up to straighten it, feeling the tears well in her eyes again. It was so painful to realize it was Papi's death that had made this horrible scene possible.

"So this is a meth lab," Elias spat out.

"Sure looks like it," Armando agreed. "Look! Here's the actual stuff." He pointed to a plastic bag of brown crumble. "Do you think we should take this down with us?"

"No, better leave it the way it is," Elias replied. "The sheriff will want to see it. This is a big-time crime scene."

Andorra wiped her eyes. "I don't want to see any more." The thought of the bedrooms made her gag. "Let's get back to Nick. I don't know what would have happened to me if he hadn't been here. I'm sorry I'm so weepy. This whole thing is really getting to me."

"Don't apologize, *mijita.* It's hard to see Aaron's house this way. And Lloyd. What can you say? You know? I remember when Aaron had him up here runnin' the cows. Couldn't been nicer to him if he was his own boy. Think of him doing all this."

Jimmy stomped up the steps of the porch. "*¡Hijole!* What a mess!" he exclaimed as he joined them in the kitchen. "I think Lloyd got away. I don't see blood or anything."

When they came out of the house, they saw Nick sitting in the door of the barn with the shotgun across his knees, still keeping an eye on Vince.

Jimmy marveled: "Man! I heard that guy was some artist. Sounds more like he's The Terminator. I guess you didn't need us much after all."

"He was brilliant," Andorra said softly as they walked to the barn.

"Think we should bandage up that foot?" Nick asked. "He's losing some blood." They stood in a circle around Vince, staring at fragmented boot and oozing flesh.

"Don't you touch my foot!" Vince said through gritted teeth.

"He's not going to bleed to death. Just leave it." Armando shrugged.

"How you gonna get me outta here?"

73

"We'll put you on your horse—we should make you walk," Jimmy said. "Wait a minute, this is Moises Griego's horse! Remember he was around asking if anybody had seen her?"

"Yeah, that's right. It was a mare?"

"Absolutely."

"Well, meth is one thing, horse stealing is another," Armando said, laughing.

Andorra lifted the lids of the feed containers—all empty. "This horse is hungry. I don't see any grain or hay. I wonder if they were letting her out to graze. And there doesn't look like there's anything but a pack saddle here."

"He can go bareback. We'll just bridle her," Armando said.

Soon the mare was ready. Vince was boosted to her back, cursing as his wounded foot hit the horse's rump and struggling to keep his seat.

Andorra uttered a little cry. "Wait! I have my father's ashes. I want to bury them up near the spring. I can't go without doing that." She bit her lip. "Why don't you start down? I won't be long."

"Andorra, we're not going to leave you alone after what happened," said Elias.

"Do you mind if I stay with you?" Nick asked. "I

74

can help you dig." Elias, Armando and Jimmy exchanged glances.

"No, no, I can manage. Oh, what am I saying? Thank you, Nick. That would be kind."

"I'll make sure she gets down all right," Nick said to the group. "We'll probably catch up. There might be another shotgun around—"

"It's by the house," said Armando. "Jimmy, there were some shells in the kitchen."

"Good. We could keep one in case Lloyd shows up and you can take the other," Nick said as he looked up at Vince's hate-filled face. There were horns tattooed on both sides of his forehead. He was just as glad he hadn't noticed them before.

Jimmy was back in a moment with the shotgun. "Here's the shells. I've got some candy bars too." He dug in his pack and gave a Milky Way each to Nick and Andorra, which they ate ravenously on the spot while he loaded the shotgun.

"Thank you all for coming." Andorra put her hands on Elias's and Armando's arms. "I'll never forget it. If we don't meet on the trail, I'll give you a call when I get home. Give my love to Elvira. I'll be over to visit soon."

"Okay. We'll get this guy out of here, Andorra.

You hurry down."

"Aaron was a great guy. Say a prayer for me."

"Me too."

"Let me shake your hand," Elias said to Nick. "We're really grateful to you, son."

Armando slapped him on the back.

Jimmy grinned. "That was really cool."

"Thanks. Thanks. I was glad to help," Nick said.

Andorra's friends waved as they headed toward the arroyo with Jimmy leading Moises' horse and his father and grandfather behind. They were soon out of sight. Andorra and Nick heard Vince yell a curse and then the silence returned. Their eyes met, full of awareness. They had survived.

"Let's get the things from the mine," Nick said softly.

As they pushed their way through sunflowers higher than their heads, Andorra reached out to cup the flowers. "My father used to grow corn here—chile too. He irrigated it from the spring. It was my job to look for worms in the ears." Andorra smiled fondly. "It doesn't take long for these sunflowers to take over." Nick watched the memory straighten her shoulders, lift her head.

"How's your jaw?" she asked, looking at the

bruise forming on Nick's face and the traces of dried blood.

"Not broken," he said, checking it again with his hand. "My teeth are fine too. I guess I have a little cut inside my lip. I must be looking like a desperado myself with this growth." He rubbed his stubbly face, tightened his lips into an approximation of a cruel sneer and waved the shotgun to make the point.

"You look great," Andorra said sincerely.

"Did the rope cut you?"

"I have a bad scrape here. How about you? The inside of your elbow is raw."

"It could be worse. What does the house look like?"

"*Couldn't* be worse."

"Definitely a meth lab?"

"Indeed."

"So you grew up with Lloyd?"

"We're the same age. When I'd come here in the summers to visit Papi, the kids ran around in a pack. As Lloyd said, we'd go swimming and hiking and inner tubing on the river. Sometimes he showed up when he wasn't too busy getting in trouble. It seems that summer up here helping Papi didn't do him much good."

At the mine, they reassembled the packs,

retrieved the shovel and the thermos, brushed the box holding the ashes clean. Nick glanced at their sleeping places. What a night. What a morning. They crawled out of the mine and Andorra led the way back toward the house.

Passing between it and the barn, they headed up the hill following the sweet sound of running water tumbling down a channel almost hidden by overhanging grasses and flowers. Above was a small, spring-fed pool beneath a grove of aspens shedding golden leaves over the lush grass. The asters were so luminous Andorra felt something inside her leap at the sight. She set the box by the spring, knelt, scooped water in her hands, and drank deeply.

"Have some," she said to Nick. "It's the best water in the world." He knelt alongside her, put down the shotgun, took a drink, and washed his face.

Andorra stood and looked at his strong back and dark head. "Nick, I have to thank you again. It wouldn't have been pretty if I had been here alone. What you did was quite brilliant."

He twisted and smiled up at her. Yes, by some stroke of luck, it had worked. He noted cerulean sky and Hansa yellow leaves framing her black hair. Wild curls around an oval of ivory and rose madder. And those dark eyes—there was art. He had nearly forgotten what it felt like to want a woman so much.

Andorra picked up the box and moved toward a cluster of boulders above the spring. Though the spell was not broken, her action gave him a chance to catch his breath as he followed. Here she was, he thought, about to bury her father's ashes and here he was with another chance to find his daughter. The trip on Saturday—Christ, he'd been up here for two days! This was Friday and he'd planned to get to Albuquerque tonight so he could catch his flight early tomorrow. No chance, he grimaced inwardly, to take his reward for having saved her.

Andorra crouched before one of the rocks, her eyes misty. "I want to put him here. See these marks?" She traced the shallow design on the side of the dark boulder. "This was our favorite place. Papi used to call it our family rock."

"Is this where you want the hole?" Nick asked quietly.

"Yes."

Andorra sat with the rosewood box in her lap and watched Nick open the earth with the shovel; he knelt to dig, the handle was so short. After laying aside a section of sod, he found the ground underneath to be fairly loose and he soon had a nearly two-foot hole. The shovel struck something.

"We must have hit a rock," Nick said, probing for an edge. "I think that's all we can do."

"That'll be fine." Andorra leaned over the opening and gently placed the box at the bottom. "Oh, Papi, I love you. I'll always love you," she whispered.

After a moment Nick helped her push the earth around and over the box, pressing it down after every few handfuls until the hole was filled. He laid the sod on top and they scattered the leftover earth among the wildflowers. Andorra made a bouquet of asters, laid them on the grave and sat quietly beside it for several minutes.

"You know," she said after a time, "he used to have me get up on a stump down at the old Duran place where we parked and look under the hood of the pickup. He'd trace the tubes and wires and show me the carburetor, the radiator, the filters. He'd try and get me to diagnose whatever problem we were having. I was pretty good.

"He taught me to shoot too, but just bottles and cans. He was a softie when it came to hunting. During droughts, the black bears would come down to eat the pears from the tree in front of the house and drink from the spring, but Papi wouldn't dream of shooting them. One time there was so much fresh bear sign every morning, we decided to stay up and try to see the bear. We waited on the porch in the shadow of the full moon and it was so cold we wrapped up in a blanket. Sure enough, a bear came and climbed into the tree. It made *such* a noise eating the fruit and snorting and breaking branches. It kept stopping and looking toward us and swinging its muzzle around in a circle, checking for a scent. You could tell it suspected we were there and it was nervous, but it stayed and ate. The night was so bright we had a great view. I always remember how safe and warm I felt under that blanket with Papi."

She got up abruptly and strode away, looking at the ground. Nick waited for a moment, absorbing Andorra's story, then picked up both nearly empty packs, the shotgun, and the shovel and followed her. She turned and took her pack and the shovel but they didn't speak again as they crossed the meadow. The arroyo now contained not a trickle of water. They walked in its scoured bottom until they reached the path that climbed to the amphitheater of sagebrush.

Earth and sky had been washed entirely clean; the blue above was deeper than Nick had ever seen at midday. Was it the sight of the sky or the nearness of

Andorra that gave him the nearly forgotten feeling of happiness? He gazed at her graceful body and again peered deep into the heavens, wishing this moment could go on forever.

Andorra glanced back at Nick who was looking up and missed it. Strange she had remembered the night with the bear when Papi made her feel that no beast could get within the circle of security he made around her. She realized that was how she felt now with Nick a few steps away. There could be ten meth labs here in the wilderness, each staffed with ten armed maniacs, and she knew Nick would get her through. She *did* feel that. So now what? Anything?

Nick had to laugh at himself. He was relishing the sense of his power, his cunning, his masculinity. He'd never had an adventure like that! This girl! Her body, her hair, her lovely smile. And when it came down to it, he had actually pulled off the rescue. Damn! He felt good—*better* for having a sore hand and knee and jaw. He could have shouted for joy, maybe with some chest beating thrown in. It was what a man was born for.

He thought again about the next step: sexually possessing the girl. There was the scene where she submits to his will, all resistance swept away by her gratitude and the realization that he has earned her favor, and there was the part where she can't withhold her response to that masculinity, heretofore noted. What was she but its feminine counterpart, as driven by her genes and hormones and psyche as he by his? Nick didn't doubt for a minute that their story would proceed in just that way from the moment he put his hand on her. A man knows when a woman is ready to play her role.

Could he just pretend for a while that relationships between men and women were that simple? Couldn't he, please? And that quickly, the euphoria was gone. Of course he could not—or rather should not—pretend that Andorra was some generic female. She was real—needy and gutsy, calm and emotional—and her love for her father was touching. Deborah was like that at first, wasn't she? Well, she hadn't exactly loved her father.

Now here he was off on another please-not-wild-goose-chase, searching for the child she had stolen from him—Christina, his beautiful treasure. How could he rest until he had tried everything to get her away from her mother's cocaine-fueled cavort to who knew where? And he wasn't due to rest, in fact, he only had hours before he was off on his latest search. Was it right to rip at Andorra's clothing, and heart, and disappear minutes later? Could he, should he, "make it right" afterward by promising to rejoin her, wherever she was, after he went to New Orleans? But what if he thought better of the involvement in the meantime, as well he might?

"Looks like they're still ahead of us," Nick said, looking out over the sagebrush and pretending his mind was occupied with no more than that.

They passed the horse in the corral around one o'clock. There was water in an old wash tub. Andorra stroked the mare's nose and said she was sure Jimmy would come back for her. Only her rental car and Nick's truck were in the parking area.

"I'm terminally tired," she sighed, "and I'd kill for a shower." She looked at Nick, her eyes serious, unguarded. "Thank you."

Suddenly his self-control collapsed. Nick dropped his pack and the shotgun, reached down and raised her off her feet with an arm under her hips. He ripped at her pack, dropped it and pulled her into a kiss. Their mouths met, already explicit with desire, and her hands came up to press him closer. In an instant their breathing was ragged and restraint was thrown to the wind.

But even while touch and taste were focused on

the other, hearing made them aware of approaching wheels and engines. Slowly, reluctantly, their lips parted and Nick let her slide down his body. Just as they turned, two pick-ups showing the county sheriff's logo roared into the yard and braked sharply.

Nick glanced at her, too disappointed to smile.

"Hi, Andorra," Levi Martinez called, getting out of the first truck. He was uniformed and looking properly serious.

"Levi. It's so nice to see you."

"Mighty glad to see you too, *hija*. Mighty glad to see you safe." Levi took off his hat and put it on again. "Look, I'm sorry about you losing your dad. I had a lot of respect for him."

"Thanks, Levi."

"And you must be Nick White. Good work from what I hear. So Lloyd ran?"

They nodded, slowly coming back to earth. "I think Vince shot at him but it seems he ran away," Andorra said.

"Would this be his shotgun?"

They nodded. "It's one of their shotguns," Nick replied.

"We'll take that for evidence." Levi picked it up and handed it to one of his deputies who put it in a pick-up.

Levi reported that Elias had called to tell what had occurred at the house and happened to catch them all in Estancia. "The boys here" were going up to collect evidence. Vince was on his way to the hospital and Lloyd,—he shook his head disgustedly—they'd get him. Adelina had been told all was well. "I'm going to need a statement from each of you," Levi continued. "If you don't mind, I'd like to talk to you now."

Nick and Andorra exchanged glances and Nick shook his head as reality intruded. "Sheriff, I'm glad to help but I've got to get on the road to Albuquerque soon and get this house closed up before I do. Can this wait until I get back?"

"I'd rather we do it now. Memory goes, you know. It won't take long. Can we go in the house and—"

"I forgot you were going away," Andorra said with poorly disguised alarm.

"I was forgetting about it myself. But it's not something I can put off." His eyes were pleading. "I guess we have to talk to the sheriff. I'd better get started."

Levi looked from one to the other; the charge between them was obvious.

"Perhaps I'll go to Adelina's and get cleaned up and have something to eat," Andorra said abruptly. "Levi, can you talk to me there when you're through with Nick?"

"Sure, honey," Levi replied.

"Andorra, I'll stop at Adelina's on my way out, may I?"

"Of course." Confused, she looked anywhere but at Nick. "I'll see you too, Levi." She picked up her pack and walked quickly to the car. Nick stared after her. What had he done? The sheriff startled him with a touch on his elbow.

"Should we go inside?"

Six

Javier sat on the rim of the fountain in the small plaza near his home, pulled the borrowed sombrero low over his face and slumped in misery. All that he had taken for granted in his life had been snatched away, his privilege in ruins around him, the laws of his universe unstuck. How appropriate that he was dressed in these poor clothes; the gardener likely only awaited their recovery before he fled to seek employ with a family of honor. He dreaded going back to that house of fear and sadness, dreaded what he would see in his father's eyes when he returned from the plaza where his grandfather—the proud, powerful father of his poor mother—would by now be ignominiously dead. How was it possible that the mighty could fall so low?

And how possible that the beautiful ritual of the Holy Faith and the raiment of the Bride of Christ, ecclesiastical displays that had been so right in his eyes, how possible that he saw them now as the actions and trappings of bejeweled murderers officiating at bloody altars? Hadn't the Holy Church thrown down the reeking pyramids—but to what end if the God of the churches built of those stones *also* demanded human sacrifice? Javier trembled and tried to push the thoughts from his mind. Surely he was risking hell to think thus.

If only he could believe what his grandmother had told him: that there was a truer faith, one that had understood God's injunction not to kill millennia before these filthy priests had perverted the truth, and that he carried that faith in his blood. She had shown no shame and insisted that he feel none—rather pride. God did not want him to be killed, she said. God would understand if he dissembled. One could keep the Commandments in one's heart and God would be well pleased.

Javier's eyes filled with tears as he remembered the last and final time he had seen his grandmother. With his mother sent away, his father seemingly thinking of nothing but the fortune at risk, his grandfather in prison, it had been his dear grandmother who had wrapped him in her love and wisdom. Javier thought of how she had tried to ease his grief on the day she entered the Convento de la Encarnación, only a month ago.

"Don't be sad that you won't see me, Javi, my darling," she had said with her hand gently on his arm. "I will be content there. I can pray always for your grandfather and perhaps my taking the veil and your poor mother's fate will be sacrifice enough. I hope good marriages for you and your sister and an honorable position in society are still possible." She glanced at Javier's sister huddled with her cousin across the room. "We must hope too, that the Church will be satisfied with your grandfather's estate and my own property that I take to the convent and will leave your father's fortune alone. I must be seen—we all must be seen—to reject your grandfather, though reject him we never will, will we, darling."

Javier had felt like a lost boy, not the manly nineteen-year-old he had recently been. She had seen his weakness.

"Remember, we are exactly as we should be, Javi. You must hold your head high. We should have told you, but we thought you were too young to understand and now you must grow up very quickly. Our lives may be taken, but never our dignity. I know it seems that we have been handed a difficult path, and I am sorry, for your sake, that God does not always offer us easy ones. Our people are passing through a dark and dangerous time in our history…" She sat for a while in silence, then lifted her head high. "Come. It is time to go."

Isabel de la Cruz rose from the love seat where she had been whispering to her grandson. She wore an elaborate dress of wine-red velvet; her arms, neck, fingers and mantilla were adorned with diamonds and pearls. She was fifty-three and very beautiful. The vast reception room held a dozen members of her family, wearing their own jewels and finery, their orders and medals and their sashes across their chests. They rose when they saw her on her feet and she smiled at them, nearly gaily, as was correct on such a "joyous" occasion.

She had held that smile as she nodded and waved from her carriage to the crowds who gathered to see the elite of Mexico on parade. The family had not entered the grand door of the convent church but had gone into a private chamber where intimate friends had been invited to join them before the ceremony began. Still smiling, Isabel de la Cruz had kissed each one goodbye and Javier had received the last kiss before she went into the recesses of the convent.

The church hadn't been completely packed

with notables as it would have been if the circumstances had been different, but its capacity had been filled with fortunate peasants who gathered to gawk at the finery of the privileged. Rockets shrieked and boomed above the church as the family took seats near a metal grill covered on the inside by a black curtain.

Javier had seen little María Inez Hernández enter this convent a year before. Then, he had ridden with his parents and sister in the parade of carriages as his sister mourned the loss of her friend and his mother scolded her for treating the occasion as a sad one. María Inez had later behaved shamefully herself, weeping during the ceremony.

At last the curtain had been drawn back and Javier had seen his grandmother in her red dress and jewels kneeling on a purple carpet with flowers scattered all around her. The bishop, priests and altar cloths had been resplendent in crimson and gold; scores of candles had blazed before a statue of the Virgin dressed in black velvet, pearls and diamonds— her gems likely carried into the convent on another woman as rich as Isabel. The curtain had closed and, after a time, parted briefly for a last look. Grandmother had then been dressed in a white cashmere gown, not with the white veil of the novice but with the black of the entirely committed nun. He could barely make out her smile through his tears as the curtain sealed her from his sight forever.

~~~~~~~~

Adelina set the plate of eggs and green chile in front of Andorra and slathered a piece of bread with butter and homemade apricot jam. She all but bolted the food, at first declining the seconds Adelina offered, and then accepting another thick piece of bread and jam. When she had finished and Adelina had taken her dishes, she laid her head on her arm and sighed.

"Oh, Auntie, what a horrible time. I was so scared." She had left out other superlatives, however: so aroused, so infatuated.

Adelina had heard the basics of the story when Armando had come to put her mind at ease a while before. She had heard that Nick White had bested Lloyd and his dangerous friend and brought her girl out safely. Of course, the experience must have upset Andorra. *That Lloyd,* and another one too. And she'd been up there all night! Who knows what had happened.

"The house, how was it?" Adelina asked.

"You never have seen anything so ugly, Auntie. I don't know how I'm going clean it or what I'm going to do with it afterwards. It might be a blessing for me, in a painful way. What I saw made it so clear that all that life with Papi is over. It's over. I think I'm going to have to sell. How can I take care of his houses and lands? Look what happened. Do you think anyone in town would want it?"

"People don't want to live so remote as La Escondida, nowadays, *hija*. And it has so much land with it. Eee, it must be worth a lot. I've been bothered ever since your papi died. I asked Jimmy to ride up a few times and everything was fine, but now, no. The big problem is the access. Octavio always wanted to put that road through Arroyo Ancho for Aaron; he loves his bulldozer so much. But Aaron wanted it not to change. Maybe it's time to put that road. Maybe it could follow the trail where Aaron took his cattle out to sell."

"It makes me sick, Auntie, to think of disturbing that beautiful country."

"The world has changed, *mijita*."

"What would Papi think if I sold a part? He was so proud that it was together. He always talked about how his father had bought land that had gone from the family."

"Maybe you could find one person to buy it."

"I'd have to sell it to someone who wanted a

95

religious retreat or something like that. Oh, I can't think about that now. I must have a bath. Levi is coming to take my statement. Eee, it will be necessary to throw these clothes!"

Five minutes later, Levi pulled up to the house. Adelina invited him in and poured a cup of coffee.

"So what did you think of Nick White?" Adelina asked.

"He's not what you expect from those artists. They were in trouble up there. I don't know how he managed. He made it sound like it was nothing, but he wanted to be sure I knew Andorra was nearly molested or killed. Lloyd has gone too far. I believe he will be in prison for a long time. White said the other one was even worse." Andorra came into the room.

"How are you, *chica*? Better? Come sit down. I want you to tell me everything that happened."

Andorra took a place at the kitchen table. She looked considerably improved with her clothes changed, her hair washed and curling around her face, and her back straight. She glanced out the open door toward the parking area and back to Levi.

"Okay, let's go. Where do you want me to start?"

The story was clearly of the same incident, but

her version emphasized Nick's bravery and boldness. Adelina listened with a growing understanding that Andorra's life might have taken a new direction; she noticed the repeated glances toward the lane. Finally, Andorra stood up and looked out the door as she told Levi how Nick had fought with Vince. She was pacing back and forth across the kitchen when she finished.

Levi looked over his notes. "Are you going to be willing to testify, Andorra? Kidnapping, illegal substances, maybe attempted murder?"

She sighed. "I suppose so. I'd like to think Lloyd wasn't as bad as Vince. I wonder if he ran away because he didn't want to kill us, and Vince did. I don't know how else to explain Vince coming into the barn with the gun. How is Nick's face? How did he look when you left?"

"He's got a bruise. He was in a hurry to get ready for his trip, throwing stuff in his suitcase, and wanted to finish his statement quickly. He'll be okay."

"Did he finish packing while you were there?"

"No, he looked like he had more to do."

"So he hasn't left yet?" Andorra asked, walking to the door and opening the screen a few inches.

"No," said Levi with a glance at Adelina. "Andorra, we haven't seen you here in a long time.

Where are you living now?"

"I'm in London. I've just finished school and I'm thinking of teaching history, but first I want to write a book about the Conquest and the Conquistadors who came to New Mexico."

"London? Do you believe you'll make it back to testify if we get the evidence for an indictment and trial? Of course there's a lot to do and we'll have to keep in touch."

"Where are you going to search for Lloyd?"

"Armando went to see his mother to tell her what he has done and make certain he isn't there. I don't know how Lloyd came from such a good woman."

"I wonder if she'll blame me if I testify against him."

Adelina shook her head. "How is that possible, *hija*? Lloyd has bothered this valley all his life. She knows that. Having that gun? Tying you up?"

"But I don't believe he would have killed us, Auntie. Will Nick have to testify too?"

"Yes, I think so. We have to see what evidence the boys bring down and we have to find Lloyd. Okay, I am finished. Thanks for the coffee, Adelina. Do you have a cell, Andorra?"

She gave Levi her number. They discussed how

long she'd be in the country, he wrote down a contact in London and Andorra walked him to the pick-up.

"How is your family, Levi? I'm sorry I forgot to ask."

"My boy is in Iraq. He was in the Guard."

"Oh, no."

"So far, so good."

"And Sarah?"

"She has two girls now. The baby was born last month. The most precious thing in the world."

"Give her my greetings and my best wishes to Levi Jr."

"Yes, thank you. Goodbye, Andorra." Levi got in his pick-up. She watched him drive down the lane and turn onto the road. You could almost forget you were in the United States here, she thought, until the military came calling.

The sky was beginning to put on one of its afternoon spectaculars as the sun sank toward the mesa. Her mother had made sure their travels followed the circuit of culture, beauty and fancy resorts: Provence and Tuscany, Mallorca and Ibiza, Thailand and Bali. When it came to skies, however, none matched these— none.

A Turkey Vulture swooped low over the house;

Andorra spun to watch it climb to join the kettle circling above. About forty vultures made the valley their summer home. One day soon they would be gone from the skies over Estancia, off to Mexico for tropical wintering, but now they were holding their evening social, wafting up and up the columns of rising air, peeling off to skim the cottonwoods, taking one more ride and then another. Tonight they would sleep together in a tree by the river—always the same one— and tomorrow after a morning flight like this, would scatter over their vast territory to watch for Death to set the table. She had heard they arranged themselves on a grid; if one descended toward roadkill or stillbirth, the vacancy in its coordinate would alert the adjacent birds, which would in turn descend, signaling others by their absence, until the tribe was gathered and feeding. It had always seemed like the perfect life to Andorra: sleeping in the bosom of family, alone with your thoughts during the day.

At last! She heard a vehicle enter the dirt lane leading to Adelina's house and turned to see Nick's white pick-up. He drove up beside her, got out and leaned against the door. His clean-shaven jaw was visibly bruised; he cupped it and smiled carefully.

"Pretty sore but not as bad as it could be. My

hand's worse. Good thing I'm not a pianist. I guess I'll be able to board the plane without scaring people too much."

"So it's off to New Orleans? One of my favorite places."

"Mine too. I hope the good times will roll. They will if I can find my daughter and see that she's all right."

"Will you try to bring her back?"

"That's what I want. I'm really worried about the life she's living but I don't even know if she'll be there. I've had lots of disappointments. My private detective had better be right this time or… I don't know what I'll do. Take over his job, I guess."

He didn't make eye contact and Andorra's heart sank as she realized he was saying more than a temporary goodbye. It appeared their time had slipped away and his mind was on another girl. She wasn't going to make a fool of herself if she could help it, but how she wanted to grab his arm and plead, "Don't go! Take me with you! Come back to me! Don't forget me!" Maybe he would come back, but with a child. It would be crowded.

"Well. I wish you luck, Nick," Andorra said, distancing her heart. He was leaving and that would be that. She'd probably be back in London by the time he returned. "Again, I don't know how to thank you. How do you thank someone who has saved your life?"

He bowed. "You exaggerate, but it was my pleasure. Given that it turned out all right, it was a pretty damn good adventure." He glanced at the house. "I need to give Adelina the month's rent. She's there?"

He had come to give Adelina the rent?

"Of course," Andorra said, crushed anew. She walked toward the house and pushed the screen to find Adelina picking chicken off the bone for enchiladas, conveying studied unawareness of the scene in the yard.

"Nick needs to talk to you about the rent, Auntie." She barely kept her voice steady and Adelina knew immediately that something was wrong.

Nick greeted Adelina and accepted her thanks with gracious self-deprecation. He offered her a plastic bag containing most of a quart of milk, salsa and olives that he had taken from the pick-up, recited his travel dates, said that they well could change, and promised to call and let her know. "There's some extra here," he said, pulling an envelope from his jacket pocket. "I'm hoping you can get someone up there every few days to check on things, though I imagine it will be pretty quiet around here for a while."

"I guess you've taken care of that, Mr. White," Adelina smiled, feeling guilty for her warmth while her dear girl was so clearly unhappy. How was it possible that a man could overlook Andorra? What a mercy he'd been there and what a shame he was leaving.

Andorra walked to the counter and poked at the chicken. She didn't look at Nick as he chatted with Adelina about his plans to get the paintings crated, transported to Santa Fe and shipped to Germany.

"I may have more days of painting or I may come back and feel it's time to stop. It's a good idea to let them rest, so I'll see when I return." Andorra sensed he was talking to her as much as to Adelina, but he wasn't saying anything she wanted to hear. Nick seemed nervous, speaking fast and repeating himself. How different from his reluctant speech as they shared that first coffee and talked about his failed marriage and lost daughter. I know he likes me, Andorra thought, but it's clear he's not going to get involved. And it's probably for the best.

Andorra swung around with a weak smile. "Nick, you'd better get on the road if you're going to Albuquerque. Be sure to drive carefully. Have you taken any pain medication? You're not going to get drowsy, are you?"

"Just some over-the-counter stuff. I'll be all right but I'll be glad to hit the bed tonight. Goodbye, Mrs. Sandoval. See you soon. Walk me out to the car, Andorra?"

As they approached the pick-up, Andorra saw the two of them reflected in the window. Nick's arm rose, hovered over her shoulder then fell back to his side. It made her remember the kiss. Apparently he was thinking of it too.

"Andorra, I apologize for...you know. I don't know what to say."

"We don't need to say anything. I know what you have to do. I hope you find your daughter, for her sake and yours. And we'll dine out on our adventure." She tried for a gay smile but imagined hearing the awkward questions at that dinner table: "And where is that fabulous man now, Andorra? When will we meet him?"

"Yes, a fine adventure. I'm sorry, but Christina has to come first. That's her name, Christina. May I call you and let you know how it goes?"

"Absolutely. I'd like to hear. Adelina always knows how to reach me. Off you go now. Take care." Andorra knew sadness was imminent. It was time to stop this goodbye. She backed away from the pick-up, raised a hand and turned toward the house. Nick stared after her for a moment, climbed into the cab and started the engine. He was nearly across the yard by the time she reached the door and quietly closed the screen behind her.

Seven

Andorra had been right about the need to be careful; exhaustion set in long before Nick reached Albuquerque. It was 8:30 by the time he had checked into the hotel, requested a wake-up call for 6:15 and collapsed in his room. The drive had given him plenty of time for thought, but most of it confused and unproductive. His mind had lurched from Christina to Andorra and back again.

He was terrified at what he'd find at the address on Royal Street. The number was two blocks beyond the Cathedral; he could picture the first block—the side of the Pontalba Apartments, the wrought iron balconies—but couldn't quite remember the second. Wasn't there that grocery with the door opening diagonally on the corner? Wait. Was he thinking of Chartres? Right, Royal was behind the Cathedral.

Hank Green, the detective, had told him—Could it have been only four days ago?—that Deborah was there and that he thought she was using again. He'd said he'd seen Christina too, and that she was dressed in very short shorts and a midriff-baring blouse. Nick had broken into a cold sweat at the description. She was reaching her teens. *Please let me find her this time.*

And what about Andorra? One moment he'd been ready to ravish her, the next he was telling her he was sorry. She'd clearly been put off by their goodbye at Adelina's house. Hurt, more like it. God, he should have left her alone. She was lovely—just don't think how lovely—but he was on a mission and Andorra would have to be a missed opportunity, at least until Christina was sorted out. Was she a girl who'd be waiting when you finally got around to her? She'd said she wanted to know how it went in New Orleans; I'll see how she acts when I call, he thought. The next second he was nearly gnashing his teeth over the image of little Christina, no longer so little, with at least one drug addict in the house. Andorra was eclipsed.

In the morning the hotel duly woke, fed and transported Nick to the airport. He tried to suspend thought on the trip; a chatty seatmate on the first leg and a nap on the second almost let him pull it off. He was in New Orleans by two o'clock and getting out of a taxi at the corner of Royal and Dumaine at three. The number was halfway down the block beside a green door covered in deep craquelure. He knocked and waited. No answer. He knocked again. Still no answer. Suddenly he was pounding, putting all his rage and pain and longing into the blows. Calm down, he ordered himself. Maybe they were out shopping. He turned to look for a place to wait and saw Hank Green—in a beret, for chrissakes—running up the block toward him.

"I tried to call you! They're gone! They got away yesterday! I'm sorry, man."

For a moment, it occurred to Nick that the pounding might be satisfyingly transferred to Hank's face, but the fight went out of him before it could surface. He looked at the detective in the preposterous beret with weary eyes.

"Don't give up, man. I know where she went!" Hank panted, out of breath from his run. "They went to the Bahamas, to Bimini! They were booked to Alice

Town on North Bimini but I think they're going to stay on a yacht at South Bimini. I been doing my homework, man, and I been to Bimini. I got some great informants with the airlines. There's a guy over here two doors down, been watching for me. Okay, they surprised me, him too, but before she left, she told him she was off with her friend—Chuy, Chuy Felix—and they were going to stay on this boat. He says she went on and on about how fancy it was, an' he says hey it's hurricane season, an' she says that doesn't worry her, they'd just go to Havana if a hurricane came, an' he says they hit there too. And he didn't call me for two days. Go figure. Anyway, man, that's where she is, her and your daughter, and I'm going to head over there next week, see what's what."

"Fuck that, Hank. We're going tomorrow, or at least I am," Nick snapped. "I'm out of my mind with worry. I can't risk letting this trail get cold. And what's with this informant? You let me think *you* were here. Exactly who was it describing every detail of what Christina was wearing?"

"Yeah, yeah, well, that was him. He seemed real reliable. I was here but I had to go back for this health thing I had to deal with. You know how hard it is to get an appointment and—"

"Hank, if this is fucked up again..."

"Believe me, this is fixable. Let's go get a beer. Oysters? How about the Pearl? I'll get us tickets to Miami and we'll see how soon we can get over to the islands. Sure, sure, I'll go with you. Just pay my ticket. I'll give you the time. I feel rotten about this. I just knew we had 'em. Your wife, she has some kind of sixth sense. No barnacles growing on her, that's for sure."

Hank Green puffed his way beside Nick through the French Quarter to Canal Street. At the restaurant, the late-lunch crowd had thinned. Soon they had a couple of oyster po-boys, cold beers and tickets to Miami for 9:30 the next morning. Hank had worked his cell phone and Nick his credit card. Nick's spirits had picked up when they parted with plans to meet at the airport.

The morning after she said goodbye to Nick, Andorra woke determined to push him and the events at La Escondida out of her mind. She would go to Santa Fe and immerse herself in the documents she needed for her research. The comforting quiet of libraries and the old deeds, grants, diaries and letters written in the Spanish her father had insisted she speak and read— these were her therapy when times were tough. There was the tantalizing chance of finding something overlooked for decades or of correcting a critical mistake in a previous translation, and her familiarity with the terrain, place, and family names of the area gave her a special advantage.

Her mind would be too occupied to lament what was not to be. She would be back in England and he would be…somewhere, who knows. Maybe he was just another damaged guy. That was likely why he was divorced—if he was divorced. Had he actually said he was? A bad sign, a divorced man. A worse sign? A not-divorced man. He'd have to be partially to blame for the marriage failing, anyway. It always takes two, doesn't it? Was Papi partially to blame for his divorce? Andorra didn't actually think so. No one had ever stayed married to her mother. She'd had a couple of other marriages no more successful, and shorter.

Nick had a child, anyway.

Truth be told, Andorra was right to doubt her heart. She was intelligent; she was a fine student; and she was hopeless at understanding relationships. Harry, her last boyfriend—perhaps her very last she sometimes thought—had been a nightmare. So desirable when she met him at the university, all tall and dark and besotted with her—she had never wanted to leave his bed—but then he had begun to imagine that she was flirting with his best friend. When he accused her she laughed out loud it was so far from her thoughts.

"You laugh at me?" he roared and Andorra had stood up tall.

"Yes, I laughed. I love you, you idiot."

"I won't be your fool, Andorra," Harry had said as he grabbed her upper arm and twisted the flesh. His eyes had looked crazy and mean and Andorra hadn't seen it coming for a second. His behavior became worse and worse until, thank God, he was called up for military service and shipped out to Basra. She'd carefully played the devoted girl back home until he was gone, and then had changed her e-mail address and phone number and instructed their mutual friends, upon pain of death, to say they hadn't seen her. She was half convinced *her* death could have resulted if he hadn't been taken away.

Her confidence collapsed. Endlessly thinking over everything Harry had said to her, she still couldn't decide if there had been clues and, in the fear he'd convince one of his mates to beat her up, she took to triple-locking her flat and had an eye hole installed. It had been a relief to move Papi in, as though her shuffling, silent father could have protected her.

Andorra was well trained in making poor romantic choices. She could never forget the scenes as

113

her mother's unpinned couplings separated, one after another. She had been pulled from her bed at night to make an escape, listened to hysterics outside a locked door, watched her mother try to get revenge with lies, even to the police. Papi had not been chosen for his sweetness, Andorra was sure. His dark good looks, his outdoorsman sexiness, his property... Yes. But his fine character? No more than useful for her mother's purposes. She had only cared about money, looks, style, a title—no matter how shaky its provenance. She certainly had had beauty and sparkling wit to offer in return, but loyalty? Hardly.

And what good man had she herself been attracted to, Andorra thought? If she had been ready to jump into bed with Nick it was practically proof of something awful happening at the end of the day. And if she found a good man, he'd just want children. She'd refuse and he'd leave her, or she'd agree and get her chance to wreck a child's life.

Andorra's mother, Jane Trevellyan, had known how to keep her audience in the palm of her hand and impressionable little Andorra had attended far too many performances. In her hunger for security, she had taken criticism or neglect as her due and, even when she achieved those visits to her father, she'd never questioned that she had to get on that plane and go back. Her mother had always called the tune.

Jane had met Aaron when she was very young and very wild. The event occurred on a summer trip to see the American West: cowboys, Indians and, surprisingly, the Hispanic descendents of the Spanish Conquest, Aaron among them. They met at a dance in Taos; they drank themselves into bed—or rather into a sleeping bag in a convenient teepee. The next day Aaron took Jane on the long trip to his adobe house where an actual bed awaited. They hardly left it for days and often returned to it as a substitute for the night life, restaurants and parties Jane was accustomed to, and increasingly missed as time passed. When she found she was pregnant, Aaron's vast properties and successful cattle enterprise made marriage seem like a not-unreasonable idea.

But what would become of her and the baby if anything should happen? She needed assets in her own name; it was only natural with responsibility growing inside her, she claimed. Aaron did all she asked to calm her anxiety. Soon she had her own well-stocked bank account and parcels of land. He was surprised to discover they were being sold as fast as they could be turned over, but he was too fascinated by his English Rose to think critically about their future or the likely result of her accumulations.

Aaron was forty-five when Andorra's birth changed his life from one day to the next. He had delighted in his sister's children but his own was a gift beyond giving. Life was full of relatives and friends coming up the arroyo, rejoicing with him that he had finally made a family. Jane could relate to some of the hippies who lived in and around the village, but Aaron's relatives never warmed to her or she to them. More and more she hated the work: water to be hauled from the spring, pinto beans endlessly on the boil, trimming the wicks of the kerosene lamps, and the nappies, sweet Jesus, the nappies. Aaron loved to make a party on a bright fall day when he slaughtered a calf—the *pièce de résistance* being nearly raw slices of liver passed around with beers cooled in the spring. Jane found it all disgusting.

What on earth had ever drawn her to this primitive life? She was distracted when she was getting stoned with her hippie friends but as her husband turned into a sober father, Jane couldn't remember what she had ever seen in him. And he talked about another child! Aaron took over more and more of her work. Soon

Andorra was on the front of the saddle as he rode out to check the fences; she chattered adorably as he cooked dinner; she curled at his side as he read a bedtime story—while Jane was in the apartment she needed in Santa Fe, or in London, ostensibly to see the parents for whom she never had a kind word.

Eventually, Jane thought she had enough money to compensate for her foolish choice: a two-mile horse ride, for pity's sake, to get to a house that was worse than a hovel and to a husband who thought assisting a cow and calf through a difficult delivery made for scintillating dinner conversation. Or more likely breakfast conversation, since he would have been out the entire night!

One day she was gone, and Andorra with her. Did she want the child, want to spite Aaron or did it not even enter her mind that she would break his heart? Andorra, just seven, had no idea what was happening to her. Jane was off to new adventures, all to be played out in luxury, her lesson learned. *As God is my witness, I'll never go two weeks without a massage again.*

Aaron drank himself through a depression that ended only when Andorra finally came back.

"I'm going go to Santa Fe tomorrow morning,

Auntie, but I'll come back for lunch on Sunday. I need to get to work. Dr. Obregon knows I'm in New Mexico and I need to see him. I think he's going out of town next week."

"That's a good idea, *hija*. You will still see my boy when he brings the family on Sunday," Adelina said. It was clear to her that Andorra was going to be brave but even so the girl wouldn't want reminders of what had happened, both the scare and the brush with love. She needed her work to distract her.

"They found Lloyd," Adelina reported when Andorra called on Thursday. "He passed a red light in Española. They took him to jail."

"That's good, I suppose."

"Nick hasn't called."

"Oh, really?" Andorra said breezily and went on to tell about her week in Santa Fe.

"It's been two weeks and Nick isn't back," Adelina casually mentioned in another telephone call.

"Is that so?" Couldn't she stop going on about it?

When Andorra wasn't lost in her piles of yellowed documents, she had begun working through the conundrum of what to do with her New Mexico properties. There were about two hundred acres around

Papi's house, two houses in town, the old Duran place, other parcels of land here and there. The buildings needed care—adobes required even more maintenance than other types—and though she had planned to go back to London once she had finished her research, now she felt she would stay long enough to put her affairs in order. Perhaps she should have that road bulldozed and get her father's house cleaned out—certainly that—and look for a renter or buyer. Mary Hernandez from Estancia was all grown up and had a real estate office in Taos; she would know what was happening in northern New Mexico, how much the ranch was worth. Maybe she should work on her book in Estancia or rent a place in Santa Fe. She needed to do some research in Mexico City before she started to write and Mexico was a lot easier to get to from here than from London.

What she didn't say to herself was that Nick would be back and that she wanted to see him again.

Nick and Hank arrived in Bimini after a miserable, frustrating wait. Three consecutive tropical depressions, unable to decide if they were or were not hurricanes, had kept them grounded in Miami for twelve days. The time when Nick planned to return to New Mexico had come and gone and he had seen quite enough Little Havana with its trendy *Cubano* restaurants and night clubs; enough Art Deco pink and turquoise; enough of Hank Green too.

At last their plane took off. Bimini appeared from the air like emeralds surrounded by sapphire pavé but on the ground, no loupe was necessary to see its flaws. The touts were desperate; hurricane season is as "off" as you can get when tourism involves going out in vulnerable little fishing boats. The cab ride through the downscale paradise of cheap hotels, strip malls, golf courses, dive shops and rental boats made Nick more depressed by the minute. All charm seemed to have gone with Hemingway's beloved hotel, the Compleat Angler, when it burned. That had probably been a dump too, he thought sourly.

Much to Nick's annoyance, Hank disappeared before he could put his bag in his room and get back down to the lobby. When the detective returned a few hours later, the news was bad. No red-haired woman with a teenage daughter had been here—not on regular flights, not on charters, not on any boat that had checked in with the harbor master.

"Maybe they went straight to South Bimini," Nick said hopefully.

"Yeah..." Hank sounded dubious. "No

international flights go there directly and everybody already knows this Chuy character, but, yeah, we should go and see. There's a water taxi that can run us over."

"What are we waiting for?" Nick asked with a sigh.

South Bimini was no better. Nick got to follow Hank around as he worked his information-gathering tricks, but no one had seen Chuy, Deborah or Christina. A young woman with the harbor police said Chuy Felix's friend with the boat was Carlos Villarrubia, *persona non grata*, suspect in a nasty beating the previous year. His boat was in the marina, empty. Hank had been right—there definitely was a Bimini connection, but most likely the storms had caused a change of plans.

That evening, Nick hunched over a beer in the Monkey Business, the bar and restaurant attached to the hotel. It was hot and the closest thing to air movement came from the waves of bass pulsing from the juke box. "Wasted away again in Margaritaville…" Idle fishermen at the next table were obnoxiously drunk and a woman on a bar stool seemed to be having trouble keeping her shorts from working into her crotch. She glanced invitingly toward him between episodes of ostentatious laughter at the barman's witticisms. Soon she was sure to need him to buy her a drink. Hank was due down for dinner and Nick was trying to decide what to do with him next.

Hank appeared but didn't make it past the woman on the barstool for some time. She reached out and tugged at his beret and he adjusted it with an attempt at a seductive smile. Finally, a glance toward Nick reminded him about his gig and he whispered something in her ear—his room number, Nick supposed, cursing his luck at being next door. Hank jostled the table as he took a seat.

"Whaddya think, boss?" he yelled over the music. "You want me to figure out what's next? I'm feeling as bad as you are, believe me."

"I doubt that. I'm wondering if she's getting tipped off. Are you sure you're careful? She's damned smart."

"Nah, she doesn't know. Man, was she always like this? Here today and gone tomorrow?"

"Pretty much. You don't think that neighbor in New Orleans told her?"

"I told that guy your daughter was kidnapped. He thought it was a bum deal. He wouldn't tell her."

"Maybe he acted too interested."

"Yeah, maybe."

The bartender brought over two menus; they

both ordered grilled fish. While they waited, Hank recounted previous successes in investigating errant wives and bigamous husbands and Nick drank another beer.

"Look, I'm off to bed," he said when he'd finished his dinner. "Don't get in any trouble. We'll talk tomorrow about what's next."

He couldn't sleep. The air conditioner rattled as though a fair portion of its parts were flying around inside the rusted metal box. Earlier he had shut it off and tried to keep cool by opening the sliding doors to the balcony, but the sounds of Hank's predicted encounter were given easy entry and eventually he resorted to the air conditioner again.

The loop of his favorite scenes started round in his brain: Andorra nearly naked in the firelight; Andorra sleeping sweetly beside him, moving against him as though she was begging to be his. One smooth leg glided across his hips; she slid her graceful hands down his body; again she took off her jeans and this time her panties too. A deliciously wanton Andorra slipped her tongue in his mouth, straddled his hips and took him inside. It was just as well she wasn't really there, he thought, when he could think again. He would have disappointed her with the speed of his response.

Sleep still did not come. Yes, perhaps it was just as well that he was not pursuing Andorra. She was a puzzle—not wanting children? A hard position, and he *had* a child, or hoped he would again…someday.

Family. He thought of how eagerly he had "taken the plunge." After all, marriage hadn't looked hard for his happy parents and he had the most beautiful woman he'd ever seen. His friends thought he was nuts, not for choosing marriage, but for choosing Deborah, and of course, they'd been right.

She had been torture almost from the beginning: the engagement ring wasn't showy enough, nor the honeymoon in Italy. He'd thought he was doing pretty well; his paintings were being collected and the better galleries were taking an interest. So he wasn't able to offer the *palazzo* in Tuscany but what had been wrong with that charming *pensione*? Where had Deborah gotten her ideas of entitlement and when did it come about that he owed her and could never give her enough?

He remembered how happy he'd been when she got pregnant, though it had not proved to be an intimate time; she had been too uncomfortable and grouchy for tender moments. Still, for a while, things had seemed better, hadn't they?

Nick knew he was supposed to figure out what part was his fault. Okay, he was obsessive when he felt the work was flowing. He'd always had those times when he dropped out of the scene, shutting himself in the studio and working until he was exhausted and there wasn't an olive left in the fridge. He'd be gone for weeks from the nightly attendance at whatever bar or restaurant was in vogue, and not start coming around again until he'd finished the series or the show. He remembered those alcohol- and coke-fueled friendships and rivalries—half the time, backbiting and snide; the other half, all for one and one for all, with people who knew the terror of putting the colors of your soul and the design of your intelligence out there for all to see.

When he came back from one of his creative binges, Deborah would be waiting in all her Pre-Raphaelite beauty: that red hair down her back—the reddest hair he'd ever seen. He remembered the night the painters had called out names of pigments that might capture the color, while Deborah smiled her haunting, distant smile. There were hints that she hadn't waited alone while he was immersed in his work, but he'd dismissed them; he'd thought he couldn't live without her. And he'd been faithful! There was his life lesson. He pushed women from his mind and eventually slept.

The next morning, Nick poked at his eggs, black beans and plantains while he waited for Hank. The food looked Cuban but it was not nearly as good as in Miami. Cuban food. Havana. It suddenly struck Nick that Hank's informant in New Orleans said Deborah considered Havana an alternative in case of a hurricane. Of course, those tropical storms had been all over the Caribbean, but if she and Chuy did intend to go to Cuba, there was another issue. You couldn't go there directly from Miami—anti-Castro sentiment had seen to that. You went via Mexico.

Eight

Cloud shadow was reworking the vista by the second as the horses made their way down a steep hillside and around scattered piñons and junipers. Andorra was in the lead and Jimmy behind her. She pulled up part way down, stood in the stirrups and looked both ways along the slope.

"This is pretty iffy here, don't you think, Jimmy? Could you get down with one switchback or would you need two?"

"I think we'd better find another place. This dirt's too loose. Any road will wash out first downpour."

"Okay. Let's go back up." Andorra pulled her horse's head around and urged him up the slope at a shallow angle. A jackrabbit made a run for it and the horse tossed his head and snorted. "Easy, Homebrew," Andorra crooned.

Five minutes more along the top of the ridge and another possible route presented itself. A long, gradual slope eventually reached the arroyo that wound its way into the distance. Andorra felt sure that the ridge on the far side would be the one behind Papi's house; hadn't she ridden this way in the old days? They surely were close. The trail to the house and meadow had to be just beyond that turn in the arroyo.

Andorra had finally made her decision. She was putting in the road, not from the village of Arroyo Ancho where Octavio lived with his bulldozer, but despite the difficulties in the terrain, from outside Estancia. She and Jimmy had been scouting for three days, carrying bundles of stakes with day-glo orange ties for marking the route. She'd give Octavio the job but she wanted to choose the path herself. It wasn't easy; she and Jimmy had started over a couple of times, but whatever the difficulties, she had decided to drag the homestead into the twenty-first century—first with this road, then electricity, a holding tank and pump, a bathroom and perhaps another wing on the house.

In fact, she didn't ever need to sell it; Papi had taken good care of her. She would spend the year building and writing. The book was outlined; she knew the holes her research would have to fill. It made her happy every time she thought of her projects.

They rounded the curve in the arroyo, but the trail to the house didn't appear. "Darn. Looks like we have to go farther. How many miles do you think we've come?" Andorra asked.

"Four, maybe five. It's hard to tell with the twists and turns. Wait! Look there, Andorra! Isn't that the tower you see behind the house?" He pointed to an eroded column of rosy sandstone in the distance.

"Oh, yes! That's it. We did it, Jimmy! I'll call Octavio tonight and see if he can ride out with me tomorrow and approve the route."

Andorra sat at Adelina's kitchen table, drying her hair. "I'm so excited, Auntie. It's a good road. I believe my father would have come to like it too. Auntie? Do you hear me?" Andorra took the towel off her head, got up and looked outside. Adelina had gone to the edge of the lane with a sack of garbage. The phone rang.

"Hello."

"Mrs. Sandoval? Oh! Is it Andorra? It's Nick."

"Oh, Nick. Yes, it's me," Andorra said with forced calm. "How are you?"

"What are you doing there? I was af—I thought you'd be gone."

"No, I got myself involved in various things. Where are you?"

"I'm in Miami. I wanted to let Adelina know I'd be back tomorrow. I know I've been gone longer than I planned. Did they get Lloyd?"

"Yes, he's locked up."

"Great! I'm glad he won't be any threat."

"Was your trip successful?"

"No, it wasn't. I'll tell you all about it. That is, if I see you. Will you be in Estancia?"

"I should be around. I hope we can get together."

"Yes, see you soon."

Was that casual enough? Andorra hung up the phone, sat down hard on her chair, rubbed the towel against her hair and stared blankly. Idiot, she said to herself. That call was for Adelina, not you. He thought you were already gone and he'd let you go. He did sound nervous but maybe that was because he realized he was going to have to see you again. Perhaps right now he's trying to figure out a way around it. Andorra put her head down on the table. Now where was her joy over her projects?

Adelina came in the door. "What's bothering you, *mijita?*" she asked as Andorra raised her head, looking strange.

"Nothing. I was feeling tired after going to town."

"Truly?"

"Uh—and Nick just called. He said he'd be back tomorrow."

"Well, that took a long time. Did he find his daughter?"

"He said he didn't."

"Poor little one. Did he say more?"

"Like what? What more would he say?"

"You *are* tired."

"Forgive me, Auntie. Let's not talk about Nick."

Andorra tried to remember what she was feeling happy about when the phone rang. Oh, yes. The road. Octavio had finished his work the day before yesterday and she was very pleased. It had done minimal damage and had made access to some extraordinary country. At La Escondida, it ended in a parking area behind the barn and corrals, with the spring, the meadow, the wooded slopes behind the house undisturbed. Her excitement took over again.

"Let's drive out tomorrow, Auntie. I can't wait for you to see the road. The country is so beautiful. I'm going to have Octavio bring me some loads of base course for the steep parts. I'll see what else I'll need after the snows."

Andorra chattered on. She had drawn up plans with her cousin, Patricio—Pat. He was a contractor now and, luckily, had been available. His crew was cleaning and would soon install the electrical and water systems followed by the bathroom. The electric co-op had come in with a bid for poles and wires so high that Andorra had decided to go with solar. Pat had done installations in Santa Fe and assured her they could easily power lights, a computer and a pump; Papi had left her more than enough money, and it would be good not to have wires even though there would be no telephone. One had to go nearly to Estancia to connect with a cell tower so she was investigating satellite systems for phone and internet.

Though Andorra didn't know how La Escondida would fit into her life, she felt she was honoring her father by tending to the old place. There was the vague hope too that the project would suture the wounds made by her mother's casual thrusts—the wounds that somehow never stopped bleeding. Could healing come from going to school, writing a book, building a road or nourishing the roots her ancestors lives had spread deep and wide? What was Archimedes' assertion—With a place to stand and a lever long enough, one could move the world? At least she would have a place to stand.

Nick landed in Albuquerque, reclaimed his rented truck at considerable expense and noted warmly the "Land of Enchantment" slogan on the license plate. Even following the next-to-useless trip, he found some comfort in returning to this place.

As he drove north, he considered the next steps in his quest. Hank had thought the Mexico/Havana idea was a good one and he'd started working his sources. Chuy was from Mexico City and reportedly, close to his family; he traveled frequently between Mexico and the U.S. Hank thought he could use a Mexican friend to find out if he had been around in the last weeks. Nick had to admit the guy was occasionally useful.

The Berlin show was getting closer—it was already October—and would require his focused attention. A sudden pang made him grip the steering wheel. What did the fucking show matter with Christina out there? But what paid for the search but the fucking show? He had to keep all the balls in the air, no other choice.

On top of all this, Andorra was still in Estancia. If he were smart, he'd just let her be. They'd been powerfully attracted but attractions were a dime a dozen; she'd likely forgotten him. He only had to make sure that the case was going forward—the thought of those evil creatures being free and going after her! Whatever it took, he'd come back and testify. Yes, definitely he'd have to see her to discuss the case.

But what did he know about her, really? They'd barely said, what, a thousand words to each other? How many words went with drinking that coffee, hiding in the mine, drying their clothes by the fire? Nick felt a jolt of pleasure in his groin. Oh, for God's sake, he was just horny. He'd find someone in Berlin. No better city for casual sex. The women would be thin, dressed in leather and have their fingernails painted black; he'd be at the top of his game with his show a success—and it would be; there were already pre-sales and a museum acquisition. Damn. He had to get those paintings to Santa Fe to be photographed for the catalogue. The gallery had been begging for them a month ago. New Orleans, Miami and Bimini were practically vacation time.

It was evening when Nick passed through

Estancia. He saw a light at Adelina's house but didn't stop. He'd check in with her tomorrow after he had looked at the paintings. He wondered if he'd have time to do another. There was a new image in his head—a rock with an odd petroglyph floating in an azure sky, falling aspen leaves. Would the paint have time to dry? Dieter had said he wanted eight or nine in his usual size and he already had nine. Perhaps he'd give it to Andorra. Was that the Andorra he was barely going to speak to again and then leave forever? What an ass he was.

In the morning the paintings looked even better than he had hoped. Nick listed the sizes of the canvases so that he could order the remaining crates from the carpenter and send dimensions to Dieter. He loaded his two favorites in the sample crate he'd had made to check the builder's work and wrestled it into the truck. If he got to town early enough he could call Dieter at the Berlin gallery and look at his e-mail in the little newsstand off Canyon Road. He also could call Hank— no, too soon to call Hank—and get over to see Gerard at the gallery to get his recommendation for a shipper. He should buy some heavy-duty cardboard boxes for sending his paints, brushes, solvents, extra canvas, stretchers and the like, to Scotland. Maybe a call to Guy in Scotland too. Yeah, a call to Hank after all. No time to see Adelina today. He'd get an estimate from the carpenter on when the crates would be ready and then he could tell her how long he'd need the house when he saw her, maybe tomorrow.

Three days of self-control later, Nick knocked on Adelina's door. She appeared quickly and welcomed him back, holding the door for him to enter. He accepted a cup of coffee and sat at the kitchen table.

"I think I have my paintings finished and I can probably ship them in two weeks or so," Nick told her. "Will it be all right to rent the house through November? I'll only be here part of the month."

"Yes, that's fine," Adelina said looking at him closely. Lord, what a handsome man. Wouldn't he and Andorra have beautiful children, she thought. "I think it will be fine. We should really ask Andorra, though. It's her house."

"Her house! I had no idea," Nick exclaimed. "Is she around to ask?"

"Yes, she's out at La Escondida. She just had a road put in and she's there with her workers cleaning the house after that terrible thing up there. You could drive out and ask her."

"Mrs. Sandoval, is she going to be all right? I mean, is she in danger?"

"Ah, thank you for thinking of that. Vince is gone off to prison in Texas. Lloyd's going to be in jail until the trial. His family is sad and ashamed and they've been helping her with the clean up. I worry about her living alone out there after she fixes the place—it's so far from everything—but what can I do? She's not afraid. She is her father's daughter."

"She's going to stay in New Mexico? I thought she was going back to London."

"No, I'm so happy. She's going to be here for a while."

Adelina gave Nick directions to the turnoff. "You'll be fine after that. It's about five miles." She smiled as he drove out of the yard.

Nick found the cut leading off the main road. His truck bounced along and spun its wheels briefly where the ground was loose, but didn't get stuck. Piles of uprooted piñon and sagebrush had been pushed to the side; vistas were broad and empty of human presence; the smell of the sage came through the open window. At one point, the road skirted a convocation of ancient cottonwoods called together by a spring. He pulled over to enjoy them. The bark twisted, undulated, and split over the still-growing cores, looking as though it had been inscribed with runes. *There* was an image for a painting.

At last the road crested a ridge and he found himself looking down on the familiar cluster of buildings and corrals. Five men sat on stumps eating sandwiches and drinking from large plastic bottles near piles of adobe bricks, bags of cement and stacks of thick *vigas.* They turned toward him as he drove up, got out and walked across the parking area; beyond, Nick saw Andorra coming from the house. She was poured into jeans and had a denim shirt tied in a knot at her waist. Nick's eyes met hers and neither looked away, though she hesitated a moment before continuing toward the group. The workers looked back and forth between Nick and Andorra, feeling invisible.

"Hello, Andorra," Nick called as she came closer. He remembered the onlookers and said hello to the group but barely could take his eyes off her. She looked like "What Every Playboy Wants on His Construction Crew." Had she been that beautiful the last time he saw her?

"Hi, Nick. How'd you find us? Did Adelina send you out?" Andorra felt her usual Nick-inspired panic.

"Yes. Yes, she did. I wanted to talk to you about the old Duran place."

"Do you want to see my house?"

"Sure. Yes. Absolutely."

"Oh, excuse me. This is my *primo*, Pat—my cousin—and Ned and Lee and Al and Ricardo: my trusty crew. This is Nick White."

The men nodded greetings.

"That was you up here with Andorra, right?"

"The whole town's been talking about you."

"Lloyd, he's my cousin. He used to beat me up every week or so until I grew."

"You sure as heck grew!"

They laughed and continued to eye Andorra and Nick.

"The guys just hauled out the meth mess and now they're starting on the bathroom foundation. How many loads was it? Four big ones?" she asked.

They nodded.

"Lloyd never did keep his room clean."

Andorra smiled and led Nick toward the house while the workers continued their witticisms and laughter.

The sunflowers now stiff, spindly stalks topped with the spiky balls that once had been the flowers' centers. No doubt seeds were falling to guarantee next fall's glory. Aspens, white-barked and leafless, were outlined by the deep green of the pines;

flames of Virginia creeper licked up one of the porch columns and ran most of the way along its length. Dark berries on the creeper were being attacked by magpies whose tuxedo-crisp black and white flashed with electric indigo and purple as the light played over them. A page in the book of the seasons had turned.

Plastic drums and trash no longer littered the yard and porch; packed earth and gray boards were swept and firewood was stacked near the door. Beside one of the columns, a pitcher bristled with dried grasses, shards of pueblo pottery nearby. Bent-willow chairs sat side-by-side halfway down the porch.

"I remember you didn't come inside that day," Andorra remarked as they entered the first room. "We've painted the walls and cleaned the stove. This is a Majestic." She gestured proudly to the blue enamel and chrome cook stove that dominated the wall opposite the door. "They're prized these days but mostly for decoration—it's not so easy to cook with wood. I believe it's over a hundred years old."

Nick thought the room was charming. The burnished chrome of the stove glowed; beside it, a tin washtub held wood chopped to size for the firebox. The walls were a deep yellow and terra cotta tableware filled open shelves. The cabinet that held the sink, and the rustic table and chairs, were painted cobalt blue to match the stove's enamel. Andorra led the way to a room off to the right.

"You can see I haven't done much besides restoring the kitchen. This was a bedroom, but I'm going to take out the wall to the next room—also a bedroom—and make a big living room. We've put some of the furniture in the barn for refinishing. I think Lloyd and Vince might have burned the rest." The room was swept but the walls were still dirty. "I may open up a door to the porch. Double doors with glass to let in the light? What do you think?"

"Hmm," Nick said, assessing what size painting the room could take.

Andorra went back through the kitchen to a room on the other side. "I'll keep this a bedroom and the bath will be on the far side of this wall. We'll put a door about here. I think I'll eventually put a wing beyond the living room with another bedroom and bath and maybe an office. These old houses are just room after room, with the porch used as a hallway. No doubt the design has its flaws in the winter, and I do remind myself that I haven't been here in winter since I was a child, but it's traditional and I like it. Also, no matter how bad the weather, I'm always glad to be forced outside—the silence, the smell of the air, the moonlight. I'll miss quite enough not going to the outhouse, once the bathroom's in."

Nick was caught up again. The ancient house; the new plans that respected the old; the observations about interior and exterior—Andorra kept saying things that resonated with him, being aware of her surroundings the way you had to be if you were a painter. And she was right about going outside in all weathers. He had learned that at the old Duran place.

"I was born in this room. My mother never stopped complaining that while she was in labor she had to go to the outhouse in the snow. She actually told the story to David Niven once in Gstaad. He adored it."

They laughed, both a little nervously.

"I thought you were going back to London. How is it you're here doing this?"

"I began by dealing with what happened here, with the meth lab and all, and I suppose I got carried away. And I'm researching a book—I can't remember if I told you—about the Conquistadors, here in New Mexico? I've spent some time in the archives in Santa Fe and Albuquerque, though I'm not finished. I need to go to Mexico City too. You know, the Spanish here came up from Mexico. There are documents there—I suspect, I hope—that could fill in what happened, especially in the church archives. I'm studying *converso* Jews who were driven out of Spain by the Inquisition; went to Mexico; were followed there by the Inquisition; and eventually fled to the end of the earth—*Nueva México.*"

"What are you saying? That these very Catholic people were actually Jews?" Nick and Andorra had gone back to the porch and were sitting in the willow chairs as they talked.

"Yes, some of them. Some families have passed down the knowledge, others have suspicions. There are Stars of David and menorahs on some tombstones, a mezuzah was discovered on the door post of a closet in a house over near Las Lomas, and people will say their grandmothers secretly lit candles on Friday nights. Hardly anyone keeps pigs, which is strange in such a rural area. They raise goats, cows, horses, chickens—but no pigs. I wish I'd asked my father about it."

"But all the churches, the saints…?"

"The best cover was to look like a devout Catholic, right? Not that the church wasn't wildly successful around here. The Indians took Spanish names and accepted saints' names for many of the pueblos—Santa Clara, San Ildefonso, Santo Domingo, San Juan. Picuris didn't change its name but is Catholic enough to

143

insist on its right to the feast day of Saint Anthony over the claim of the Spanish town next door. I'm sure many of the crypto-Jews—that means hidden-Jews—eventually saw themselves as Catholics."

"My family wonders about our name. My father's side originally came from Germany and 'White' is 'Weiss' in German. Sometimes that's a Jewish name. I might try to check it out someday."

"All that is interesting, isn't it. What would you think if your family turned out to be Jewish?"

"I don't know. I wouldn't mind—lots of smart Jews out there."

"And now it's safe enough. There was a time when it wasn't."

"It wasn't safe for Daniel Pearl."

"No, you're right. It wasn't." A magpie let out a screech. The birds had ignored Nick and Andorra and continued to flap and fight over the berries on the crimson creeper. She gestured toward them. "They're actually drunk, you know. Those berries ferment on the vine and that's when the magpies get interested. Otherwise they're eating the dog food. Lloyd's dog is still around here. He has to spend most of his time guarding his food bowl."

"What's happening with the case?"

"Moving slowly. Vince turned out to be wanted for parole violation in Texas and he was sent back to prison there. Lloyd's in jail, awaiting trial. He was denied bail. His whole family came over and apologized to me and Auntie, and his brothers came up and put in a couple of days cleaning."

Nick suddenly bent double and began to shake with helpless laughter. "Human sheets!" he sputtered. "Did you catch when Lloyd said that?"

Andorra couldn't resist joining him, and it was a while before she could speak. "Aww, poor Lloyd. Stop it, Nick. Don't make me laugh. He never was very bright. I'm sorry it came to this for him."

"I keep seeing the four of us blundering down the trail with sheets over us. No one would have suspected a thing." Nick collapsed again, taking Andorra's composure with him. "Whew," he said at last wiping his eyes. "Sorry. But I have to be glad he's not around anymore. I was pretty worried about that."

"I don't believe he would have really hurt me, or you, but Vince was another matter."

"Lloyd gave you quite a punch in the ribs."

"I was well and truly bruised, but that was all. He gave you a nasty blow too. What must you think about us here? Really, it's usually a very peaceful place. But seriously, Nick, I'm concerned about Lloyd. I think the prosecutor is going to charge him with attempted murder and, first, I don't think he did more than assault and kidnapping—quite bad enough—and, second, I think he's actually retarded and not fully responsible. Anyway, I'm not going to testify against him on an attempted murder charge."

"It might be a hard to defend him after he tied us up."

"I know, but I don't think it's fair."

"Okay. I'll go along with that, if and when I testify. I see your point."

"Thanks, Nick."

Amazing girl, he thought. Really decent. And she thought he made a graceful cup of coffee. Then he remembered his mission and his intentions.

"So, Andorra. I've gotten my schedule together. I think I can get my paintings shipped in about two weeks and that will close out my stay in Estancia. I'll probably leave sometime in early November but, of course, I'll pay the month. Adelina told me it's actually your house. So, is that okay?"

"Yes, of course." Andorra looked at the floor and then up, smiling. "I hope your show goes well and that you find your daughter. It's been nice meeting you. I'll always owe you a great debt. Don't hesitate to collect if there's anything I can do for you, though I can hardly imagine what that might be."

"Just now you could let me take a picture of the place where we buried your father's ashes."

Nine

Back in Santa Fe to reclaim his paintings from the photographer and visit the internet café, Nick received important news from Hank Green. Not foremost, but crucial, was the word that he was off the job. He had been diagnosed with prostate cancer, was going to have surgery, and was panicky that he'd be incontinent or impotent, or both. Almost lost in the analysis of the relative merits of various approaches to therapy, given his age, PSA and biopsy results, was the news that he had tracked Chuy, Deborah and Christina to Mexico. They had been in Mexico City two weeks ago and now were in Acapulco, though that was all he knew. He apologized. He hoped to be of assistance later, but there it was. His life had taken a sudden turn. He'd be sure to keep Nick informed about his prostate.

Nick gripped the edges of the table, sloshing his cappuccino into the saucer. The chase was on again. He had to get to Acapulco immediately, never mind that he'd be on his own and his only Spanish words were *cerveza, tequila* and *escondida*. He'd damn well manage. He had the time, while he waited for the crates; he called up a travel site and typed furiously.

On the way home, he bought wine, asparagus, salmon and two perfect pears. He had invited Andorra to dinner so that he could give her the gift he'd worked on all week—the painting of the rock with the unusual petroglyph that rose above her father's resting place.

He'd put a magpie on top and another at the base and was pleased at how lively they looked—all it had taken was a small sack of dog food and an hour of sketching the ensuing melee for him to get a feel for the birds. Painted in tones of cobalt blue, French ultramarine blue and mauve, the rock floated against a transparent white laid over a pale phthalo blue background. After Andorra had told him of her research, the idea to combine Spanish gold with golden leaves had occurred to him. At the top he had made coins—*escudos*—of gold leaf that gradually changed into cadmium yellow aspen leaves falling over the scene. Some had landed on the rock and others around the lower magpie. A few gilded leaves at the base of the rock brought the reflectiveness of the metal farther down the canvas. It was good that he'd finished it given the news that was sending him to Acapulco.

Andorra had accepted the invitation with some reluctance, but had managed to convince herself that it wasn't a date but rather an opportunity for Nick to tell her the latest news about Christina and, of course, it was Christina about whom she really cared, sight unseen. How could the story not tear at her heart? Scenes of life with her mother continued to surge into Andorra's consciousness since she heard the tale and she was having little success in pushing them away.

It was already dark when Andorra arrived at the old Duran place. She wore a modest jersey dress of midnight blue, with long sleeves for the increasingly crisp evenings, and a shape that defined her breasts and hips. She carried a bottle of wine and a bouquet of the cosmos that were still blooming against the south wall of Adelina's house. The Indian summer was holding, though it couldn't be much longer before winter arrived.

Nick had made the room cozy with a fire in the wood stove. His wine was already breathing; he poured some into stemmed glasses he'd bought that day with the groceries. As she sat at the rustic table, Andorra described the bathroom's progress, while the baking salmon filled the kitchen with a thick, rich smell and water for the asparagus came to a boil on top of the stove. Nick put the cosmos in a canning jar on the windowsill since the table needed a kerosene lantern as centerpiece if they were to see their food. The room's lamplight found auburn highlights in Andorra's hair and painted her skin with gold.

She exclaimed over the smoke rising from the lantern's glass chimney. "Nick! You don't know how to trim your wicks!"

"That's the truth. I have to wash the soot off my chimneys every day."

With scissors he fetched from the studio, Andorra showed him how to cut the wick across and nick the corners. The light flamed bright and clean.

"It was my job to trim the wicks when I was with Papi. I was so proud of my wicks. I'm *quite* the wick expert." Andorra was annoyingly adorable, Nick thought.

During the meal he told her that Deborah and

Christina were likely in Mexico.

"That's wonderful!" she exclaimed. "When will you go? Where are they?"

"Acapulco. I have a flight day after tomorrow. I'm a little nervous because, frankly, my Spanish is nonexistent. I guess I'll have to find someone who's bilingual and can help me navigate the terrain. I have a notion to find the town's trendiest night club and wait in the parking lot. Deborah doesn't do her nightlife half way."

Perhaps because they were into the second bottle of wine, Andorra gave in to her impulses. "Nick! I'll go with you! I have to go to Mexico anyway and I can help you with your Spanish in Acapulco and when you don't need me I'll head up to Mexico City and do my research. That is, if you'd want me."

"Of course I would! No, wait. It might not be a good idea. It could be dangerous. I think Deborah's using cocaine again and I don't know anything about this guy she's with, but it can't be pretty. For all I know he's down there visiting his best friend, the kingpin. Christ, for all I know he *is* the kingpin."

"It would be more dangerous if you don't know what people are saying, wouldn't it?"

"Maybe."

"You're talking about danger for me when Christina is in the same situation and I could help you understand whatever is happening? First things first."

Nick sipped his wine and stared at the table, finally looking up into Andorra's expectant eyes. "Okay. You're incredible. Let me buy your ticket. Can you go on Wednesday?"

"Sure, why not? But I'll get the ticket. I was going anyway. You can pay for a hotel room with a great view of the bay. Have you been there?" Nick shook his head. "It's really beautiful. It's not full of movie stars anymore but you can certainly see why it used to be."

"When they see you, the town will think they're back." He smiled as Andorra rolled her eyes. "No arguing. I'll get your ticket and the room. And here's something else for you. I didn't realize how appropriate it would be." Nick rose from the table, opened the studio door and brought the painting into the light. Andorra jumped up at the sight of it and gave a cry.

"Oh, that is so beautiful! That is so thoughtful! No one has ever given me anything I could love more! I will treasure it forever!"

"I'm glad you like it. I'd like it to dry a little longer. We'll take it out to the house after Mexico, okay?" Nick tore his eyes away from Andorra's delighted

154

face. Now more than ever, with this trip coming up, he needed to keep his distance. Otherwise, it could be terribly awkward, and he had to watch those cracks about movie stars.

"That's why you wanted the photo! That magpie looks so, what? Knowing. I love the coins and the leaves!"

Nick collected the dishes from the table, hiding his elation at having pleased her. "My flight for Mexico City leaves at ten. I imagine I can get you on the same one. I'll get the ticket tomorrow and we can figure out when we should leave for the airport."

"Nick, that painting. I can't think of anything else. If only my father could have seen it. Think how beautiful it will be in the house." She turned toward him, but Nick looked away and picked up the wine bottle.

"Here, let's drink to our adventure. One last sip."

"To Christina!" Andorra smiled. They drank. "Now I'm off. It was a fabulous night. Thank you a million times."

Nick opened the door letting the night air barge in.

"Ooh, I'm going to run to the car," Andorra said as she reached up to kiss him on the cheek. In a flash, she was out the door. He watched her go as the air made the flaming wicks dip and dance. His cheek was already cold.

Nick hadn't been able to get Andorra on the same flight. He had arrived in Acapulco four hours earlier and had had enough time to be accosted by every tout in town, see three hotels, and make a decision. He couldn't see investing in the private pools or California King beds—not a romantic getaway, after all. Instead, he chose a charming older hotel about midway around the bay and booked two rooms on the ninth floor "penthouse." The bay was just as beautiful as Andorra had promised.

Back at the airport, waiting for her flight to arrive, Nick read the tourist brochures for the town's nightlife. There were three promising clubs: two in the Zona Dorada and one at Las Brisas where the grandest hotels were too. Had he been too modest in his choice? Maybe Andorra was used to the best and she would think he was cheap—Deborah certainly would have— and he easily could have afforded better. What *was* he thinking?

It appeared that the clubs didn't open until ten but, knowing Deborah, he shouldn't expect her until at least midnight. Yikes! Here was one with its big show at

4:00 a.m.

He glanced at the board. The seven o'clock plane had landed. Maybe a rest, dinner at the hotel, then drinks and tapas at the clubs. Would Andorra have the clothes to get them beyond the rope line or did she need the right clothes with a face and figure like hers? Maybe she'd let him buy her something short, shimmery and expensive. Christ, was he ever going to sleep with her?

There she was! Andorra emerged from the companionway looking cool and unwrinkled. White pants, a nearly see-through blouse and silly silver sandals. When did she get her toes done? She was perfect. She had left Estancia far behind.

"Hi," Nick greeted her. "Good flight?"

"Yes, since you put me in first class," she said with a grin.

Andorra met Nick in the lobby wearing a floor-length black silk dress with spaghetti straps and a necklace of pebbly moonstones. It seemed entirely possible that she wasn't wearing any underwear; a man might well spend the evening trying to decide.

She glided behind the waiter toward a table by the edge of the terrace where the sand began its gentle slope to the sea. Nick followed, aware of a certain buzz among the diners at Andorra's appearance. She ordered a Martini and coconut shrimp—Nick chose a Margarita and rib eye with pear/chipotle coulee—and then she was all business. She had Nick read from the brochures; they looked at the pictures of the fanciest clubs; Andorra quizzed their waiter; he called over the maître d'; and they decided to start at La Palma Plata—The Silver Palm.

"I'll work the bathroom and find out what places the girls are talking about. We might have to go to two or three. I hope I can stay awake! I thought we might want to find out where the upscale teens are spending their days. Does Christina have money to belong to the shopping set? Will she be lazing by the pool at a posh hotel?"

"I doubt that we can hope she's home hitting the books," Nick said, frowning.

"If she is, it's the best of all possible worlds, but would make her a lot harder to find."

At 11:20 they emerged from the taxi after a wait in a queue—this was clearly one of the hot spots. The doorman passed them to a host who accepted the six hundred peso cover and the two hundred for himself and asked their seating preference. Andorra leaned close to him and said, *"En el rinconcito más oscuro."* In the darkest nook. Their plan was to see without being seen; Nick put on his dark glasses.

"*Claro, señora. Adelante.*"

A palm frond in a silver vase sat on a table of brushed steel, along with floating tea candles and heavy green napkins wrapped in silver cord. Smoking paraphernalia—a green glass ash tray and elegant matches—was on hand for those guests who thought they were going to live forever. Judging from the haze, that was almost all of them. The band was playing something like *Cubano/Flamenco* fusion and was spectacularly good. The waiter appeared immediately and took orders for mojitos.

They surveyed the room. The younger women were Paris Hilton clones in elaborate makeup, short skirts and platform heels, except darker and plumper— this being Mexico—and the young men wore dark silk shirts under black suit jackets, their necks hung with gold chains. If they hoped to look like upscale gangsters, they were doing an excellent job of it. There were also tables of older men in well-tailored get-up, but with faces that wouldn't have looked out of place in a corn field. Their women's generous figures bulged from flamboyant evening wear.

"So tell me what Deborah looks like," Andorra

said, sure it wouldn't be like them.

"She's nearly as tall as you and was always very thin and she has this incredible red hair that she wears—or used to wear—straight down her back with little barrettes to hold it." Nick touched his temples and frowned.

"Did Christina get her hair?"

"No, hers is dark like mine. Deborah's pale skin though."

"What happened? I mean, how did you get into this mess?"

"Let's see. We were painters together in New York. She was quite good; I liked her work but she always said mine made her feel like she was going nowhere. I'd try to talk her out of it, but the truth is the art world's lousy for a woman, and after we married, she gave it up and started focusing on my career, making me a hot property. We would be seen on the town, have the right clothes, go to the right places."

"You'd be this beautiful couple on the society pages," Andorra said with a smile.

"Exactly. That was supposed to sell pictures and sure enough, it did. Only it didn't leave any time to paint pictures. She resented my time in the studio; even having Christina didn't slow her down.

"She took over schmoozing buyers and galleries, and I painted with Christina in her crib or crawling around on the floor. She'd bring buyers to the studio and talk the talk. When she finished, my paintings looked like the most significant work since Picasso's. Usually she brought the wives—often they're the real buyers—but it was the husbands she really knew how to work. I guess she was working them in more ways than one."

"Oh, dear." Andorra wrinkled her nose.

"One day I found out one was buying more than paintings, though at least he did get two before Deborah took off with him. I was doing well, but nothing like he was—he was CEO of a hedge fund. And his poor wife... I guess he figured he'd had her for more years than was appropriate at his income level. She couldn't hold a candle to Deborah, anyway. The prick paid for his divorce *and* Deborah's. I barely got joint custody with his lawyer making me out to be drugged and disorderly, which was pretty hard to take since the shoe was on Deborah's foot."

"That sounds awful. I take it she's not with him anymore?"

"She was married to him for about three years. He bought her a gallery in SoHo and she did pretty well with it. She didn't get any of the bigger names, but she does have an eye and she drew an impressive stable of hungry Young Turks. I heard she had something of a casting couch. God, she really knows how to self-destruct. Sheldon got wind of it, and to make matters worse, she got deep into coke. I guess the coke was doing the thinking."

"Where was Christina in all this?"

"We were sharing her. I'd have her in the studio or we'd go to the zoo or the park. She loved to draw; I have a great collection of her stuff. All she wanted to play with from the very start was crayons or paints. At six she won a contest with a drawing of bumper cars. She's a natural. She'd sleep over sometimes and I'd have her whenever Deborah was traveling. Even when it was Deborah's turn, I'd pick her up from nursery school and we'd talk and have a snack and her nanny would come for her later. Deborah divorced when she was about five. Surely you don't want to hear this," Nick said with a sigh.

"It's actually rather interesting in a heartbreaking sort of way. What happened next?"

"Let's see. Deborah remarried. Her gallery hung on for a while, then it failed. She got clean for lack of sufficient funds to keep her nose stuffed, I guess. Her husband was okay. He liked Christina and he and I traded her back and forth pretty smoothly. Deborah was with him for about five years, more or less. Then it was, 'Mommy didn't pick me up at school again, Daddy. I got in trouble because my gym clothes weren't clean. Larry pushed Mommy and she said we were going to go away.' We had conferences and talks and confrontations. I began to suspect that Deborah was using again and I met with a lawyer about revisiting the custody issue. Then one day Christina didn't show up after school; she didn't answer her cell phone; her mother didn't either. When I talked to Larry, he said they were gone and he didn't have a clue. The police were useless. And this is the best chance I've had since, but I don't see Deborah."

"Hang in, Nick. I think I'll go find out what the talk is in the ladies room." Andorra put her hand briefly on his and slipped out of the chair. What a miserable story she thought, but that was partnership for you.

The ladies room was decorated with potted palms and fairy lights. Several aging attendants dressed like French maids awaited their tips for handing over towels. Andorra positioned herself beside two girls chatting in Spanish and applied fresh makeup. They were talking about the boyfriend of one who was paying too much attention to another girl at the table. It appeared he was risking being unmanned if he tried anything with her. Andorra found her opening when one asked the other if she wanted to go on to Baby'O or Pabellon. Definitely Baby'O. Andorra excused herself. She had heard that was a very exclusive club. Did they know if you needed a reservation?

"*Creo que no*," the one said, looking Andorra over. Certainly on the weekend but tonight, she didn't think so.

"Anything?" Nick asked as she returned to the table.

"There were girls talking about Baby'O. Perhaps we should try there."

"Okay. Nothing I love better than dancing all night. Should I go back and get my black shirt first?"

"I think it would be quite smart with that white suit. Cartel chic. Don't be discouraged. Let's pay up. And I'm glad to hear I'm going to get a chance to dance."

"Dancing with you is entirely at odds with being inconspicuous."

Baby'O occupied a ferrocement cavern that would have been suitable for Ali Baba and the Forty Thieves. Andorra chatted up the doorman, getting closer to him than Nick found strictly necessary, but gaining admission. He had the privilege of paying out nearly another hundred dollars to be escorted to a table. Green and blue laser lines crossed the ceiling and a mosh pit resembling a colossal, pulsing jellyfish held the center of the room. They huddled at another corner table in nearly impenetrable darkness; Deborah could be next to them and it would take a while to realize it. More mojitos were served.

Nick peered around the booming obscurity— nothing, nothing, no Deborah. Then, a glance toward the door and, *bingo,* just like that, *La Deborah* was making her entrance with the likely Chuy Felix waving and calling out behind her, trying to dominate the room, though it was Deborah who drew the eyes. Her red hair was now very short and had a hint of the unnaturalness of henna, but she was ravishing nevertheless. Heads swiveled toward her erect, slim body, encased from armpit to mid-thigh in what appeared to be electric-green vinyl, her killer legs in gold stilettos with ankle straps. Nick signaled Andorra, put on his sunglasses and slipped into the chair that positioned her between him and Deborah, as she and Chuy joined a table of eight, one tier up from the edge of the dance floor.

My God, Andorra thought. Deborah in the flesh was positively scary with her arrogant beauty. How did you get over that for a wife?

"There you are. That was pretty easy, not cheap, but easy," she said with a nervous laugh, pretending that Deborah didn't intimidate her and that she wasn't reminded of the slick elegance of her mother.

"Yeah. I'm a little stunned. I haven't seen her in nearly three years, and here we are. But this thing isn't over. Now we have to sit tight until they leave and Deborah's got endurance."

Two hours passed—nearly 3:30. Nick and Andorra nursed their drinks and ate some bizarre sushi containing Philadelphia Cream Cheese, kept alert by the excitement of the chase. Deborah's table seemed to require most of the available waiters as bottles of Cristal and plates of food were brought and carried away. She went to the bathroom every twenty or thirty minutes and looked glittery-eyed in between.

Nick was more and more agitated. Andorra tried to distract him with the tale of the sailing trip she and her mother took from Australia to New Guinea on a 145-foot yacht. Nick shook off Deborah's presence enough to recall sailing in Lake Superior, visiting Isle Royale, and listening to the wolf pack chorus under the stars. Andorra countered with coyotes in New Mexico waking you up at night with their unearthly cries. Nick had heard them—like puppies being murdered, he said. They checked every few seconds for Deborah's exit.

"Are you a hunter? The way you handled that shotgun—"

"What, the way I got Vince to dance? Yeah, my dad was into hunting and fishing in an upper-class sort of way—salmon in Scotland, elk in Wyoming. We went to some beautiful places but I always wanted to sketch instead of hunt. He had me do a lot of target practice, though. He thought a man should be comfortable with guns. Just as—Look! They're up!"

Deborah and Chuy were indeed on their feet, engaged in a round of air kisses from her and robust squeezes from him. Andorra had to admit he was pretty dashing in his well tailored white suit, tan shirt and mocha tie. He was dressed, in fact, rather like Nick. Heads turned as they moved toward the door.

Nick had kept the tab paid and now had only to throw a tip on the table for them to make a quick but discreet departure. Nick walked behind and tucked his face into Andorra's hair, as though whispering sweet nothings, but being tailed was apparently not on Deborah and Chuy's minds and they did not glance back. A black sedan pulled up to the door moments after they exited; they slid into the back seat and the driver pulled swiftly away. Nick and Andorra scurried to one of the waiting taxis.

"*Siga a ese coche*," she demanded of the driver— the classic "Follow that car." He gave her a surprised glance.

"*¡Rapido!*"

The taxi took off after the sedan, speeding southeast around the bay, crossing the headland where La Palma Plata's artificial, brightly lit palm trees marked the edge of the commercial area, and continuing down the coast away from Acapulco. Suddenly, the tail lights disappeared.

"He's turned off!" said Nick

"Many big houses," the driver commented as he came up and made the same turn. The road headed down, curving past illuminated villas with spacious grounds. Where permitted to see inside, they looked frantically for the sedan. Then ahead on a straight stretch, there were tail lights again; the taxi driver accelerated to get closer, following around curve after curve, descending until they were surely near the water. The lights disappeared. Again, they looked in each drive and saw nothing. Wait! Was that gate swinging shut? Yes! They heard it clang in the quiet night as they drove past.

Andorra asked the driver to turn around and shut the lights off.

"Okay," she said, peering out the window, "We have this solid gate and blank wall with statuary on top and opposite, a line of Italian cypress. We can find this place again. Let's just hope this is it."

Nick threw himself back against the seat and expelled a lungful of air. "I guess we can allow ourselves some sleep. Surely nobody will be up early here. What is this area called?"

The driver understood him. "This is Diamante Real. You want to go another place?"

"I think we call it a night," Nick said.

"Yes, let's go back. La Zona Hotelera. Hotel Elcano," she said to the driver.

"*Si, señora.*"

"*Cómo te llamas?*" Andorra asked.

"*Enrique, señora.*"

"Enrique, do you want to drive us tomorrow?" Of course he did. Andorra put his number in her cell phone.

Ten

Not the bright morning sun, the glittering bay, or the cheerful breakfast table distracted Nick from thinking about the scene in the nightclub—Deborah's sleazy display; Chuy glad-handing his way through the press of drunks; and that table of criminals flashing their ill-gotten gains. How *could* he have loved that woman? Well, he wouldn't put his life through the wringer again. He had a child; he didn't need to think of a partnership for that. He was lucky to love his work. If he could just keep focused, Christina and Art would be more than enough.

Enter the challenge: Andorra appeared at the top of the steps leading from the lobby to the patio. She wore white silk shorts printed with big pink roses and a pink cotton blouse. Her long legs were unfairly beautiful. She saw Nick at the table and came down.

"Good morning," he said. "I was just going to call you or maybe have breakfast sent up. I was afraid they were going to stop serving."

"Sorry. I slept hard except for waking up to listen to the waves. I'd think, I'll just stay awake and enjoy this, and then I'd be out again. I'd better get some food."

At the buffet, Andorra chose fruit, scrambled eggs and bacon; considered a croissant; opted for a Belgian waffle. She ordered tea, and the waiter brought it as she returned and began mounding her fruit on the waffle.

"They have whipped cream over there." Nick smiled at her impressive pile.

"Really? I'll get some." She headed off to revisit the buffet table. Nick watched her legs as she crossed the patio.

"So what's the plan?" she asked between mouthfuls. "You know, I was thinking, there are no private beaches in Mexico. Somewhere between those mansions there have to be paths through to the sea.

Once we're on the sand we can get a look inside the walls—nobody wants to block off their ocean view. Who knows? Maybe we'll find Christina on the beach."

"Good idea. Let's call Enrique. When you're done, of course."

They got out of the taxi as soon as they saw the tops of the cypresses they had noted the night before. Andorra told Enrique they didn't know when they'd need him to come back; he assured them he'd wait just out of sight. Who knows what he thought they were doing. He turned the taxi around and was gone soon after. They hiked along the street looking like vacation renters too new to the tropics to drop their compulsive exercising. Now to find that access to the beach.

They reached the walled house and walked nearly a quarter mile beyond it before the grudged pathway between two mansions presented itself. A chain was strung across it; there certainly was no law that ATVs had to be allowed through.

The beauty of the cove on the other side was stunning. Hills rose sharply around the turquoise bay, revealing here a corner of tiled roof, there a pink or yellow wall peeking from the lush vegetation. Huge rocks thrust up from ocean and beach. There wasn't a soul in sight—no, wait, some splashes of color and an umbrella could be seen far around near the point. They began walking back toward the house that they hoped held Christina, worrying that they wouldn't recognize it from the beach side.

"Look, Nick, when we find the house I'll try to get inside and see if it's the right one. No one will recognize me."

"What excuse are you going to use to get in?"

"Maybe some oldest-trick-in-the-book like I've twisted my ankle and can they help me?"

Nick looked at her slim ankle and thought how very far from red and swollen it looked.

"Too *lame?* Okay, I'll pretend I thought it was the house my friend was renting and then…play it by ear!" Andorra looked around excitedly.

Nick wished he could think of another plan. He didn't like Andorra going in alone, but Deborah had amply demonstrated her unwillingness to honor his rights and his appearance was not likely to go down well. Anyway, he had finished with unreciprocated fair dealing. He had succeeded in getting a judge to revoke Deborah's custody some months ago, and now that Christina had been taken out of the U.S. without his permission, Deborah could be charged with a crime. But he didn't want to traumatize Christina; if he could only get word to her and see if she wanted to be with him, get her to run away with him... That would be more than enough.

They passed one villa where children were shrieking and playing around the pool, but most of the houses were shuttered and quiet. Finally, they saw the statues on top of tall stucco walls that stretched all the way to the beach on each side of the property and turned with downward swoops to a low gate in the center of the ocean side. Bougainvillea weighted with red blossoms draped over the peach plaster; inside they glimpsed a terrace edged with more statuary—cheesy imitations of classic Greek sculpture. Gilded cesspit, Nick thought, gritting his teeth. Red-cushioned lounge chairs were arranged alongside a pool where an enormous rock, clearly kin to ones offshore, had been made into part of a fountain. The plash of water into the pool accented the silence. Nick and Andorra peered through the bougainvillea and nodded to each other, nearly certain it was the house whose gate they had seen closing the night before, and at that moment, Chuy walked out onto the terrace.

"This is it!" Nick whispered.

Without the fine cut of his suit, dressed in tiny

swim trunks, Chuy revealed a considerable paunch, nevertheless, he moved like a man incapable of believing that his appeal could be compromised. He reclined on one of the lounges as a maid came out carrying a tray with a cup and silvered pitcher. She put it on a dining table while she moved a smaller table closer to Chuy; he ran his hand up her leg when she got within reach. With more grimace than smile, she quickly retreated and when she returned with the tray, she served him from as safe a distance as she could manage.

A young girl with long dark hair, wearing a painfully brief bikini, stepped onto the patio as the maid went back inside. Nick gasped, "It's her! It's her!"

Christina took the lounge chair farthest from Chuy and didn't return his "*buenos días.*" She carried a book that she immediately opened and hid her face behind. Chuy's eyes were riveted to the rest of her.

"If you stare at me one more second, I'm going to tell my mom," she said, with her nose still in the book. Nick grabbed his head in his hands.

"Nobody's looking at you." Chuy turned away. "And your mom, she's already *en el paraíso* today," he grumbled. "She keep this up and one day I'm going to be all you got. An' then I teach you how to dress."

"Okay," Andorra whispered as she saw Nick color

and tense. "You stay out of sight. Here I go." Walking rapidly up to the little gate, she called out, "*Hola! Hola! Buenos días.* Excuse me, do you speak English?"

Chuy sat upright on the lounge chair and leapt to his feet when he saw Andorra. "Yes, yes, of course. Come in! Please!" He waved off a heavy-set man who had started out of the bushes at the sound of Andorra's voice. Nick jerked back around the corner of the wall.

Andorra let herself in the little gate and shook hands with Chuy who had descended the steps of the patio with considerable speed.

"I'm sorry to bother you."

"No bother, no bother!"

"I'm your neighbor...well, for the month, and I'm looking for my friends' house. Jim and Cherie? Do you know them?"

"I'm afraid not, but please come in. Have a cup of coffee! Perhaps the *muchacha* knows where their house is. If we're neighbors, we should get to know each other, no?"

Christina lowered her book and rolled her eyes.

"I am Jesus Felix Andrade, Chuy to my friends. She is Christina. Say hello, Christina," he said sharply.

"Hello," Christina mumbled, again behind her book.

177

"Christina, go ask Louisa to bring another cup of coffee. You will take coffee, *señora? Señorita?*"

"Judy. I'm Judy. Do you have tea? No, never mind. Coffee will be lovely. This is such a beautiful house."

"Christina!"

"Louisa's bringing my breakfast. You can ask her when she comes out." She glanced at Chuy, threw up her hands. "Okay, okay. I'll go." With exaggerated weariness, she dragged herself into the house.

"Tell Louisa we have another breakfast too," Chuy called after her. "You'll take breakfast, won't you, Judy?" His eyes darted about, trying to resist going below Andorra's face.

"Oh, I've eaten—well, maybe a little."

"Now, tell me," he smiled, his teeth flashing in his dark, handsome face, "what you are doing in Acapulco? Are you here with your husband?"

"Oh, no, I'm not married," Andorra laughed. "I came down with my family. We took a house over there." She gestured vaguely down the beach. "Then my friends Jim and Cherie decided to come down too. I know they're renting somewhere near here. We arrived last night, so I'm out looking for them this morning. He's tall and blond and she's short and blond. Maybe you've seen them on the beach? They've been here a few days."

Christina came back to the patio, followed by Louisa with another tray of coffee.

"*Louisa ¿sabes de algunos gringos que rentan una casa cerca?* Do you know any gringos renting a house around here?

"*No, señor. No sé de ningún gringo por aquí.*"

"Sorry, Judy. She doesn't know them, but we'll track them down. Christina, have you seen them on the beach?"

"I don't know what you're talking about."

"My friends?" Andorra said. "They're Americans. A couple? Both blond?"

"No." Christina returned to her lounge chair.

"Too bad. So tell me Chuy. What's fun to do around here?" Andorra asked flirtatiously.

"Aaah, Acapulco is a very fun town. I have many friends here. Perhaps you would like to join us in the evening for some music and dancing."

"Who's us? You and Christina?"

"Ha, ha, ha, no. Christina's *mother* is my friend. Her name is Deborah. You will like her. She is a very elegant lady like you." Chuy had no mode other than full steam ahead with a beautiful woman regardless of whether or not it would land him in trouble. Perhaps it already had.

"Chuy! Come up here a minute," a demanding voice called from above. Andorra and Chuy looked up to see Deborah leaning over a balustrade under a bougainvillea-covered arch on the second floor of the villa.

"Deborah, this is our neighbor, Judy. She's looking for her friends."

"How do you do?" Deborah said flatly. "Chuy, can you come?" Deborah floated back out of sight.

"Please excuse me," Chuy said, looking annoyed, his dignity wounded at being summoned and his fun with the exquisite Judy interrupted.

Louisa emerged from the house with a large platter of sweet rolls, butter and jams, sliced fruits and a bowl of yogurt. A teenage boy carried plates, napkins and silverware to the table and began to set it while Louisa returned to the house and reappeared with a pitcher of orange juice.

Andorra took a place at the table and Louisa poured her a cup of coffee. "Won't you join me, Christina?" she asked.

Christina looked at her sharply, hesitated, then got up and took a seat. She spooned a small amount of fruit and yogurt onto a plate while holding her open book in the other hand, making it clear that she had no interest in being social.

Andorra glanced toward the upstairs terrace. Empty. Louisa and the boy had gone inside. Without looking at her, she murmured, "Christina, I've come with your dad. Don't react. He's hiding just over there near the wall. He's been going crazy looking for you and he desperately wants to see you."

Christina gasped and froze with her spoon in the air. "Who are you?"

"A friend of his. Look, Christina, he wants to take you home with him." Andorra buttered a roll as she whispered. She glanced up and saw that Deborah had come out on the terrace again.

"Hi!" Andorra called cheerily. "Chuy asked me to share this lovely breakfast."

"Yes, Chuy's quite the host." Deborah, looking annoyed, disappeared again.

Andorra continued quickly, "He's over there." She cocked her head. "Maybe you can say you want to go swimming. Be careful." Christina sat staring at her, eyes wide.

Chuy walked out into the bright sun of the patio, now wearing a tropical flowered shirt. "Good! Do you have everything you want?" He brought his cup to the table and poured more coffee. "*¡Louisa! ¿Dónde están mis chilaquiles?*" he shouted toward the house. "I like a real breakfast, don't you? What will you eat? Eggs? *Frijoles?* You are taking nothing!" Chuy again flashed his teeth with a too-warm smile.

"No, no, this is perfect. Just lovely."

"I'm going for a swim in the ocean," Christina announced. She left her untouched fruit, took the top towel from a red pyramid in a basket beside the pool, went down the stairs and out the gate.

"She does not behave well." Chuy leaned in for this whispered confidence.

"So," Andorra said, with a seductive smile, "where did you learn to speak such perfect English?"

Christina put the towel around her neck, walked out into the gentle surf and turned to scan the line of houses. Nick was just about to show himself from behind a thicket of oleander when the guard came through the gate and stood with arms crossed, staring at Christina. Nick froze.

"What do you want?" Christina snapped disgustedly. He shrugged, apparently understanding her tone, even if not her English, but didn't move. Christina resolutely turned her back to him and kicked at the waves before wading ashore, spreading her towel and lying down on her stomach. Nick cringed at the exposure the bikini permitted; the guard gaped at it.

Andorra's laughs came again and again, interspersed with the indistinct low rumble of Chuy's voice. Eventually, Nick could hear them saying their goodbyes. A moment later Andorra came through the gate calling back, "See you then!"

She hesitated when she saw the guard, then gave him a friendly nod and went over to sit beside Christina.

"Do you like it here?" Andorra asked, her voice louder than necessary.

"Oh, yeah, sure," said the disgruntled Christina. She whispered, "Where's my dad?"

"I think it's just beautiful. Look at that blue!" Andorra lowered her voice. "He must be hiding. Don't look." What to do now? She spoke up again. "Your dad invited me to go dancing with him and your mother—"

"He's not my dad," Christina snapped, forgetting the woman knew that in her eagerness to disown Chuy.

Andorra idly drew designs in the sand. Her voice was barely audible. "We'll wait for you down the beach, that way. We'll be there all day. We'll wait as long as it takes, tomorrow too." Then, for other listeners, "I'd better be going."

They heard Chuy call sharply, "Christina! Your mother wants you. *Jorge ¿ves a Christina?*" Do you see Christina?

"Coming!" Christina shouted and rose to her feet. She walked toward the house, kicking sand, some of which landed on Jorge's shoes. She looked back over her shoulder at Andorra. "I'll be there," she mouthed.

After she watched Christina go through the gate, Andorra strolled casually down the beach, not checking to see if the guard was watching or if Nick was following until she reached the path between the houses. Looking back, she saw Nick in his own relaxed ramble. He joined her a moment later, obviously anything but relaxed.

"Damn! I thought I was going to get her. Does she want to see me?"

"Absolutely. I told her you were waiting and she was out there in a flash. I said we'd be here as long as it takes. She thinks she can get away."

"She knows to come down here?"

"Yes."

Nick looked around in frustration. "What if Deborah gets suspicious? How long before I just march in there?"

"Let's try waiting first," Andorra said. "Perhaps she'll be here any second."

Nick and Andorra made themselves comfortable at the grassy edge of the sand under the shade of a palm. Nick could lean far enough out to look back toward the house, which he did repeatedly as Andorra described the scene she had witnessed.

"Does Chuy look dangerous?"

"I don't think so. He's so full of himself. God, I've never been so slathered with charm. I'm supposed to go dancing with them on the weekend. It's hard to picture Deborah liking that."

"You saw her?"

"Deborah? Yes."

"How did she look?"

"Disheveled. Hung over."

"And Christina?"

"She clearly hates the whole scene but I don't know if it's just on general teenage principles or something more...well, clearly more. She can't possibly have any friends and she's followed by that guard. He's ogling her and Chuy's ogling her. It's ugly." Andorra sighed. Nick pounded his fist into his palm and looked down the beach yet again. No Christina.

"Is anyone there beside the guard and the maid?"

185

"There was a teenage boy. I'd guess the guard is the chauffeur."

"Yeah."

"Are you imagining leaping on them from the second story? Beating them to a pulp? A shotgun blast to the foot?"

Nick twisted his mouth. "I'm considering the groin."

"Ouch."

As the wait dragged into the afternoon, Andorra decided to go for food and phoned Enrique; the taxi glided up in moments. She returned with soggy fish tacos and a couple of tepid beers. Nick was still sitting forlornly alone; they ate in silence.

Eventually, sunset approached and still there was no Christina. Andorra had begun to berate herself over not clarifying plans for the night—after dark could be the best time for her to get away and they couldn't risk having her find only empty beach. When it was nearly dark, they walked back down the beach to the villa, careful to remain out of sight. The yard was illuminated, but they could see no lights in the house.

"Do you think they're gone?" Nick whispered, his heart in his throat.

186

"Listen. The pool pump is on, the fountain too. They must have gone out, but probably just for the evening. We could go back and get some dinner, don't you think?"

After a quick bath, Andorra joined Nick at the table where he was grimly finishing his first Margarita; the waiter took the order for two more drinks and their hastily chosen meals.

"I hate it when people say they know everything is going to be all right, don't you?"

"Normally, yes," Nick said with a brief laugh, "but if you want to say something like that, I won't bite your head off."

"Okay. Remember I told Christina we'd wait as long as it takes, and we will. We'll get her."

"I'm going back right after dinner," Nick said.

"And I'll come with you."

"No. You get some sleep. You can bring me breakfast if I'm not back."

Andorra began to protest but Nick raised his hand, shook his head and stared blankly out to sea. The drinks arrived; Nick took a deep swallow. "When do you have to start your research?"

"I don't have any schedule. I can do whatever I

please. I'm here for as long as I can help or you want me. That lunch was awful. I'll get the hotel to pack breakfast and lunch tomorrow, just in case."

Nick made a sound of disgust.

"Don't worry. We'll probably be eating with Christina."

The night was beautiful; a caressing breeze lifted Andorra's hair and waves sloshed sweetly in the Pacific bowl, but Nick was oblivious to the tropical magic and looked repeatedly at his watch.

"It's going to happen this time," he said suddenly. "I believe it. Did you see how grown up she is? She's going to be a beautiful woman, heaven help her. Her face is as sweet as ever. She's a good girl. You'll see. None of this is going to change her."

Andorra murmured agreement. Let Nick believe Christina would be unaffected, though she knew that she had been profoundly changed by similar experiences—and not for the better.

Eleven

The morning was still pink and gold when Enrique dropped Andorra at the beach. Nick, alone, smiled weakly at her and dove into the luxurious food basket. He reported that he'd had a surprising amount of sleep and had just jogged past the house where he'd seen the guard on the terrace; he hoped that meant Christina had come back. In an hour, a mother with two small children came out on the sand some distance away. She eventually noticed them and Andorra waved cheerfully. They were accepted. The day dragged on until it was time for lunch, for which the basket yielded a chicken and spinach salad and brownies.

"I'm going down there," Nick suddenly said, getting to his feet.

"Then what will you do?"

"I'll think of something."

"Maybe I should go back and say I can't go dancing on Saturday and try to talk to Christina again."

"No, I've had it." Nick stepped onto the beach.

Christina was running toward them! Running for all she was worth, swerving as the soft sand gave under her feet, almost going down and touching a hand for balance. She dropped a portfolio that she carried under one arm and snatched it up again. She saw him! She was in his arms! Nick nearly fell over as he caught her and pulled her back out of sight. They crouched on the ground and he took her face in his hands and kissed her forehead, eyes and nose. "Baby, baby, baby, baby." His voice choked.

"They took me to Chuy's friend's ranch! I was so afraid you wouldn't be here! I missed you so much! I didn't think you wanted me. Mom said you wanted me to spend time with her." Christina began to sob.

"Oh, no, no. I've been looking for you since you left New York. I never wanted to be away from you. You're so beautiful and grown up. I can't believe I'm seeing you again."

190

"Daddy, I hate it here. I want to go away. I hate that Chuy, and his friends are all awful, and I don't want to speak Spanish. I'm not going to ever graduate! I want to go back to New York and see my friends. Take me back!"

"Yes, yes, we're going to go back. Listen, I don't want to talk to your mother now. We'll tell her after we're gone. Shall we just leave all your stuff and go, and I'll buy you all new clothes and everything?"

"I got my drawings; that's all I need. I don't have any clothes for New York, anyway. Mom is going to be so mad. Let's get out of here."

"You know Andorra."

"You're not Judy?"

"No, Judy's my spy name," Andorra laughed, giving Christina a squeeze. "You're a brave girl."

"I've got you!" Nick hugged her to him again, completely elated. "Okay. Let's get Enrique."

"What's best? Is Deborah going to send Chuy and his friends to try to find Christina? How long can we wait to tell her? We don't want her to think Christina's been kidnapped or drowned, though I suppose she has been kidnapped," Andorra mused as Enrique sped from Diamante Real and back toward the center of town.

"I have to take Christina to the embassy for papers before I can get her on a plane. We need to get to Mexico City and we have to get her some clothes. She can't go home like this."

"I have some she can wear in a pinch," Andorra said. "What about this: We check out right now and rent a car—I think it's about three hours to Mexico City. Or we could get Enrique to take us. Then we can shop, you two can fly out, and I'll get to my research. Shall I ask Enrique?" At Nick's nod she jumped into a rapid-fire bargaining session in Spanish.

Christina looked from one to the other, incredulous at her changed circumstances: two adults busy problem-solving *her* problems.

Nick heaved a sigh when the trip was agreed and the price was set. "Is that okay with you, Christina?"

"Are we going to New York?"

"Not yet. I've been living in New Mexico."

"You've been in Mexico too?"

"No, *New* Mexico. It's a state."

"Oh, yeah. Is it nice?"

Nick looked at Andorra. "It's beyond nice, but it might not be what you're used to. I have to go back to pack up paintings and ship them to Berlin. I have a show there in December. Tell you the truth, Christina, I've

192

been living here, there and everywhere since I lost you. You and I are going to have to sit down and figure out what we want to do, where you want to go to school. That's the main thing."

Andorra looked out the window. Christina was the main thing and how could she fault Nick for that?

"Deborah, it's Nick." He held the little phone in a death grip and scuffed his feet on the ground. "Yes, I did it. She's with me... Well, it certainly wasn't easy to find you. I've looked for nearly three years... What *right?* Remember we had joint custody?" His voice rose in anger. "Listen, I don't care! Christina wants to be with me." He backed the phone from his ear. "Enough! I'll let you know where we are as soon as we're settled... I don't know. We have to decide where she's going to school... Deborah, she doesn't want to talk to you... She just doesn't. She's probably afraid you'll talk to her like this, don't you think?" Nick looked as though he might throw the phone. "Deborah, curb your selfishness for once. She needs to have a settled life and a chance to have friends and a good school... You aren't making any sense... You can always get in touch through Oliver... Still my agent, still the same number... No, I told you I don't know where we're going to live yet... What woman? I don't know who you're talking about... No, we're not still in Acapulco. I have to go now... Sorry, Deborah. Goodbye."

Nick stood some distance from the taxi in the hills above Acapulco and gazed toward the sea while Andorra, Christina and Enrique watched him from the car. They hadn't heard what he said but could see from the set of his shoulders that it had not been easy.

Suddenly, Andorra was aware that tears were running down Christina's face.

"Did you want to talk to your mother, Christina?"

"No, no. You don't know how bad she can be. I never want to speak to her again!"

"Oh, sweetie, it's all right. Your dad is going to do everything he can to make it better." Andorra pulled Christina over and hugged her; she cried harder but let herself be comforted. Nick got back in the taxi and looked worriedly at her while Enrique politely pretended not to notice anything.

"Is this the wrong thing for you, Chrissy?" Nick asked anxiously.

"No, Daddy. This is good." She transferred her hug to him. "Let's go now," she mumbled into his shirt.

Chuy paced across the bedroom. "What do you mean, go after her? Are you crazy? You know what *ojo de hormiga* means? I have to be like the eye of an ant, too low to see. I have to cross the border for business, you maybe notice? You think I am dragging a screaming kid with me? You think I am wanting to be charged with *secuestro*—kidnap?"

"You have people you could send!" Deborah shrieked.

"No! Little bitch was impossible to live with anyway. Never a smile. It's not enough you get all the blow you can take? You're no kind of mother. A dog is a better mother! Aeee, if my mother knew I was with a woman like you…"

Chuy paced the bedroom in fury, stepping over the pillows Deborah had thrown at him. Her eyes were red; her hair stuck up; her robe was tangled around her legs. Fucking Nick, she thought, as she groaned and sagged over on her side. Chuy stopped and looked at her, pity slowly replacing anger.

"Okay," he said, sitting on the bed beside her. "I'm sorry. Calm down, baby. Here, let's have something makes you feel good. Come on. She's better with her dad, right? Let him have the problems for a change."

He took his hand from her thigh and opened the

drawer on the bedside table.

"Come on. This will make it better."

Through the hours it took to reach Mexico City and well into the traffic snarl of the capital, Christina told her stories: She and her mother had spent time with Lou in Atlanta until he had been arrested for fraud or something; Deborah had met Hal and they had gone to San Francisco (where Nick had tried and failed to find them) and then to Europe; for a while they had been in LA, then with Chuy in San Diego, New Orleans and Acapulco. Deborah had gone to rehab and Christina had stayed with Maria, Deborah's friend. Maria was a hostess in a very fancy bar and she was Chuy's sister—that's how they'd met Chuy. He was always going to Mexico on business. He had lots of money.

Nick tried to hide his gloom while the story unfolded. Andorra glanced at him anxiously as Christina chattered on, sensing that this was just the start of the child's attempt to unburden herself of the chaos and anxiety of the last years. She watched as the weight of Christina's ordeal settled onto Nick and weighed him down, wondering if she had done the same to her father during those summers; had told him about her mother being detained in Paris and about that Spaniard stealing their money. Of course she had. And, like Papi, Nick would never lay the burden down—Andorra could see that too.

She longed to tell the child that she had suffered much the same, and survived, and life was good, but Christina was touching Andorra's greatest fear: that her mother's crazy—literally crazy—life had damaged her and that she was yet to recover. As Christina talked, Andorra was so reminded of her days wandering around Europe and Asia with her mother that memory, like a fog, came in and closed around her, dimming the sad recital or obscuring it entirely.

The hotel in the Zona Rosa in Mexico City was a peaceful respite from the madness of the colossal capital. In the restaurant, Nick and Christina talked quietly as they waited for Andorra to come down from her room. Christina wore Andorra's long sleeved jersey over too-large black pants.

"What? Just the two of us are going back? Why is Andorra staying here?"

"She's researching a book. You know, Christina, she's not my girlfriend."

"She's not? You two sure do act friendly."

"Well, yes, she's a friend. I like her a lot but—"

Andorra startled them as she walked up and sat down. "My room is so beautiful! I have a balcony and a lovely garden view."

Nick and Christina exclaimed over their room, the waiter took orders for drinks, and Nick told Andorra their plans.

"The desk made plane reservations for us tomorrow at three to give us time to go to the embassy and get Christina's papers. They've promised me they'll do it on the spot. I have her birth certificate and a court order revoking the joint custody; they say we won't have a problem. We don't get to Albuquerque until nine so I reserved a room at a hotel near the airport. I'm thinking, Christina, we'll have to stop on the way up tomorrow and buy an air mattress. I only have one bed at the house and we'd better shop for some warm clothes tonight. The hotel says there's a mall just down the street."

After their meal, they sat in an alcove and looked through Christina's portfolio.

"I just have a few things. I lost most of my stuff when we left LA."

"Portraits! I've never seen you do portraits," Nick exclaimed.

"This one is Mom. Can you tell?"

"It's extraordinary. She looks like she was in a

bad mood, though."

"Ha! She was."

"I love these close parallel lines for shading. Where did you learn that?"

"I googled Leonardo da Vinci."

"You could end up as good as he was," Andorra said, making Christina giggle.

"Oh, stop!"

"So you haven't been painting," Nick observed.

"No, just drawing. You always said it was good for me to draw. And I didn't have any paints."

"Well, you made great use of your time. I'm going to have to take lessons from you. These are really fine, Christina. Look at this." Nick slid a drawing of one of the statues at the villa toward Andorra.

"I love the way you made the surface look shiny," she said. Christina beamed.

When the drawings had been returned to the room, they strolled outside into a fiesta of jugglers, mime artists, vendors, well-dressed families on promenade, trendy youth sipping coffees at sidewalk cafés, and fancy shops bustling with customers. At the mall, Christina was outfitted with underwear, shoes, jacket, several pairs of jeans and sweaters, and was completely satisfied with the slick, Mexican look. Nick smiled as he thought of her at the old Duran place. Hopefully, it wouldn't send her screaming back to Deborah, but they wouldn't be there long. And where exactly would they be? He'd think about that later; the night was too sweet and festive to spare attention from Christina, happy and pretty in her red leather jacket.

They stopped at a sidewalk bar and café on the way back. Christina enjoyed a large ice cream concoction while Andorra and Nick celebrated their success with a glass of champagne, and then another, until Christina was yawning and the street was beginning to quiet. Nick and Christina walked hand in hand back to the hotel. On the second floor, Andorra kissed Christina good night, smiled at Nick and turned off to her room.

She stood in the hot shower, touching the wall lightly, a little dizzy from the champagne. When she was done, she put on the hotel's terry robe, turned out the lights, and opened the heavy curtains and glass doors, leaving the sheers closed. Lights from the garden wavered through a palm moving gently beyond the balcony and the curtains danced slowly in the breeze.

She waited, staring into the night, and it came— the tap at the door. Knowing who would be there, wanting him to be there, she crossed the room, opened the door and stood back for him to enter; Nick pushed it closed behind him. Thought suspended, they stared into barely visible eyes for a long moment, until he took hold of the terrycloth and pulled it from her shoulder. The robe opened, and Andorra allowed it to fall to the floor; Nick exhaled, his breath a jagged tremolo. In awe, he touched her cheek, her throat, the side of her breast, stepped in and pulled her close for a kiss that grew in intensity as he backed her across the room to the bed. Tight with desire, he hurriedly pulled and fumbled at his clothes and, in a moment, had climbed above her. As he dipped to kiss her belly, Andorra lifted her hips, twisted her cheek to the pillow and moaned.

"May I? May I?" he whispered.

"Yes, oh, yes. No, wait!"

"Here, touch. It's safe." He brought her hand to feel the condom, and his readiness as well. With a soft cry, she pulled him toward her, stretching her body eagerly.

He pushed into his heart's desire; he lowered his forehead to touch her hair and cheek; he breathed in the perfume of soap and sex. His lips found the depression above her collar bone, the hollow of her throat, the rise of her shoulder, and his hips powered his reach more insistently with each stroke, until her body let some last, soft resistance fall, and he dissolved in her acceptance, moaning "Andorra, Andorra," into her hair.

She lay with eyes closed, her sex pulsing from the sweet assault and her fingers lightly stroking Nick's arms until he slipped from her and sat back between her legs. The light from the garden played over their bodies; the breeze found places to tingle with cooling sweat, and Nick began to caress her. How did he know? How had he guessed what would please her most, what would set her to trembling, what would make her grow taught and arch herself toward him? How did he know the moment to replace his finger with his tongue? How did he manage to carry her along in perfect trust and compel her to give him, as she did in blinding joy, her most private gift?

As she cried out, he entered her again. He could feel the spasms of her orgasm, feel her pleasure via nerve fibers unsuspected, fibers seemingly reserved only for a unique, heretofore-unknown entity: Nick and Andorra. He kissed her face and eyes; he dipped into her mouth over and over, and, in between, arched to reach her breasts with his lips. Finally, he again collapsed onto her body, her pleasure having overwhelmed him, and his having carried her impossibly far away—only to find herself, by some miracle, there in his arms.

Slowly the room rematerialized. In the shifting light from the garden, they lay facing each other. Nick propped his head on his elbow and caressed her reverently, gazing on the perfect poetry of full breasts, dip and swell of waist and hip, long, long leg… His eyes and hand feasted until he felt some subtle change; the silence had gone on too long; he looked into her eyes and saw that they were not happy.

"This was a mistake, wasn't it," she said. "We were doing a pretty good job of being friends."

Oh, Christ, no! "Can't this be better? Oh, Andorra, didn't that feel exactly right?"

"Maybe that's the problem. We are friends, Nick, and I know that you don't want a partner, and neither do I."

"Oh, if I could have a partner, that is, if I knew what I was doing, where I was living…" Nick looked panicked.

"Nick, please don't assume I'm looking at you that way. Just because I'm not married doesn't mean I'm searching. You're a really wonderful guy and we've had our brilliant adventures with Christina and all. If we don't mess things up, we'll part friends and maybe we'll check in now and then. And it was great sex."

"Oh, yes! It *was* great sex. Let's not call it a mistake. Let me see you again. I've wanted you ever since I laid eyes on you. Come visit me when Christina and I get settled."

"I don't know. I think it's too confusing. It seems we *are* hopelessly attracted—but I want my life to be simple right now. I want to work on my book; I'm having fun remodeling the house. The last thing I want is to… You could become a major distraction, and then we'd just end up with hurt. We've been honest; neither of us wants a partnership, but one can't…well, I can't, be that close physically without my emotions getting involved. I won't be able to think straight if I'm wondering when, or if, I'll be sleeping with you again. So I suppose…I suppose I think we ought to leave it."

Nick was silent for a time. Finally he sighed, "If that's what you want." He stared into the distance, frowning, knowing that his hands were no longer privileged to touch. Maybe if he hadn't said he couldn't have a partner… Was it even true now that he had Christina? Christina. Was this about her? Did Andorra not want Christina?

Finally Andorra sat up, leaned over and kissed him gently on the cheek. "I'm going to take a shower. See you in the morning?"

He was gone when she came back. In spite of what she'd said, her heart sank when she saw the empty bed. She fell asleep with remarkably few tears, considering.

Christina turned over in her bed when Nick came back to their room, but didn't awaken. He longed to go back to Andorra. The sounds she had made! The memory made him dizzy. He wanted to go back and say...what? Marry me? You're the loveliest, sweetest, sexiest woman I've ever known? Christina would like her, already did, and he *knew* she liked Christina. Yes, she had sent him away, but didn't she suggest it was because she thought she might want him too much? And she was assuming he didn't want her because...because that's what he'd said. No partnerships. Maybe it was for the best. He probably could have found a girl with black fingernail polish down in the lobby and by now he'd be sleeping a satisfied sleep, not wondering if he was throwing away the best thing that ever happened to him.

Twelve

Andorra made her way through the streets of old Mexico City, delighting in one grand colonial building after another. What a magnificent place it was—as full of ancient charm as anything Europe had to offer. Eventually, she located her destination—the former Pontifical Palace—where she hoped to find the documents from the Holy Office of the Inquisition. The ornate building was set well back from the street and reached through a pretty plaza.

An enormous carved door stood open to a high-ceilinged anteroom, beyond which Andorra saw a slight man with neat white hair and moustache seated at a desk. He rose when he saw her and came forward. They introduced themselves—he as Señor Carabajal—and Andorra inquired if she could be permitted to consult the collection. He invited her into the office; she listed her credentials; he asked her to describe her research interests.

Andorra explained that she was looking for information on the *conversos*—Jews who had converted when they were required, on threat of death, to either accept Christianity or leave Spain—especially the crypto-Jews who had secretly maintained their original faith. It was known, she said, that some had made their way to New Spain, and may have escaped to remote New Mexico when the Inquisition followed them. Señor Carabajal had not heard of this theory and questioned her closely on the evidence supporting it.

Did he think the collection might contain documents naming persons of interest to the Inquisition around the time the Conquistador Oñate had gone to New Mexico? He believed it entirely possible. Charmed by Andorra and stimulated by the intellectual quest, Señor Carabajal indicated she had passed her own inquisition. She wrote a formal request to see the collection, which he dictated, and impressed him by already having the required gloves and face mask in her purse. He escorted her through interior doors into the library itself.

Her eyes rose to a remote ceiling spanned by beams surely cut from primordial Mexican forest. The windows, almost completely shuttered with paneled wood, had sills above her head and recesses that showed the walls to be over two feet thick. Below each window and within the recess, high steps allowed access to the shutters or an outside view. Andorra had seen nearly identical rooms in European castles and the great libraries of Spain.

Elaborately carved moldings surrounded the open shelves where volumes bound in dark leather glinted with gold tooling. Enormous books covered in pale parchment were identified with hand lettering in black and red on the broad spines; folios lay on their sides, edges of unbound, yellowed sheets showing between the covers. In the middle of the long room on a red carpet were a table and chairs; a heavy chandelier fitted with dim bulbs hung low over them. Andorra inhaled with delight the aroma of five centuries of antiquity—waxed wood, leather, linen paper, vellum and parchment.

Señor Carabajal pulled out a heavy chair and

invited Andorra to place her purse and notebooks on the table. Indicating a set of books at the top of a cabinet, he said, "You might wish to begin there, *señorita*. Let me move the ladder." The old man began to drag a carved, A-shaped ladder with a handrail up the side of the steps, and Andorra rushed to help him.

"You must forgive me if I do not get the books for you. I think you want those volumes with the red band. Please allow me to be of assistance if you have any questions. *Estoy a sus órdenes.*" At your command. He made a little bow. In return, Andorra insisted that he was *muy amable*, very kind. Señor Carabajal moved slowly to the door, closed it behind him and left her alone in the beautiful chamber.

She put on her white cotton gloves and face mask, climbed the ladder and tugged at the first volume. It was so heavy that she had to place its edge on each step as she descended. She lugged it to the table, opened the cover and carefully folded it back, first to brilliant turquoise and mauve marbled endpaper, then to a frontispiece printed in red and black and spotted with the marks of age and the trails of book worms.

It was in this manner that Andorra found perhaps the one activity that could take her mind off that morning's goodbyes at the hotel.

Christina had knocked on her door early and told her to hurry down to breakfast; they would only have a short time together before she and her dad had to go to the embassy. At breakfast, her chatter, full of happiness about being with Nick and getting back to the ordinary life of an American girl, had dominated the conversation. Did he have an iPod? When could she get a computer? She had to open her Facebook account and, of course, she'd need the computer for school work too. Did Nick have any of her things she'd left behind? Did he have that painting of Central Park? Of course, he did. It was hanging in his studio right now.

"Andorra, when will you be back in New Mexico? Dad said you ride horses. Do you think I could go riding with you?"

"Have you ever been on a horse?"

"Oh, yes! We used to go riding in Woodstock, didn't we, Dad. We had a friend with horses up there. I've never galloped though. He wouldn't let me." She made an affectionate face at Nick.

"I have a friend in Estancia with a very gentle horse. It might be fun for you and your dad to ride out to my house. But you know winter is going to be setting in. You'll have to hope that there are still some nice days left. Do you ski?"

211

"Yeah, I'm a good skier. We went to Switzerland last winter."

"I skied in Switzerland when I was a kid too," Andorra said with a smile. "The ski valleys in New Mexico and Colorado often open on Thanksgiving Day. Do you think you'll be there that long?"

"I thought we'd visit my parents in Chicago for Thanksgiving, Christina," Nick interjected. "Your grandmother has been missing you about as much as I have."

"Oh, yeah. That'll be nice," Christina said, looking a little disappointed about the skiing.

"Lots of years there's not enough snow on Thanksgiving anyway," Andorra said kindly, "but you can always ride horses."

Andorra and Nick had hardly allowed their eyes to meet during breakfast, but finally, as Christina settled herself in the limousine and a porter put the bag in the trunk, Nick turned to her. "Thank you, Andorra. Thank you so much for helping me."

"It didn't turn out there was much use for my Spanish, did it?"

"You know you were what made it work."

"I'm so glad it did, Nick. Christina is a darling girl and I can see you're a good father. She seems very healthy in spite of it all. I know you'll be patient if she goes through any rough patches."

"Come on, Dad!" Christina called. "Goodbye, Andorra. Good luck on your book. Hope we see you soon!"

Nick brushed her cheek with his lips. A moment later they were gone.

The sun went behind a cloud, nearly extinguishing what little natural light the shuttered windows permitted into the library. Andorra started, realizing she had been staring at the same page for a long time. Ah, but what a beautiful page, she thought, caressing it with her gloved hand.

The door opened and Señor Carabajal slowly made his way toward her with a cup and saucer in his hand.

"Señorita Sandoval, will you take chocolate?"

"There's no bathroom?" Christina exclaimed. "I'm supposed to go outside in this cold? You have to be joking!"

"Well, baby, that's the way it is. My landlady will let us go over to her house to bathe and I promise we can move to a hotel in Santa Fe if things get too rough. I wanted you to see this country before we went to Chicago."

Nick and Christina had just arrived at the Duran house. They had stopped at a mall in Santa Fe and Christina had accumulated enough clothing that they'd bought a suitcase too. She had been disappointed to hear that there was no phone or internet connection at the house but Nick had, perhaps foolishly, withheld the full extent of the primitiveness of the accommodations.

He knelt beside the wood stove, arranging paper, kindling and pieces of piñon before striking a match. After the fire flared, he closed the little door and went out on the porch for more wood. There was quite a pile, as he had found splitting wood to be a curiously satisfying activity, a good way to let his unconscious mind plan the next painting or to rest the conscious part from its worry over Christina. She had pulled up a chair near the stove when he returned.

"This feels nice. Let me put in some of that wood," she said as Nick unloaded his pile on the floor.

"Good. I'll light the lamps."

Soon the room was cozy and charming in the gentle light. Spaghetti tumbled in boiling water and Newman's Own Marinara Sauce bubbled beside it. For Christina, initial shock had given way to the fun of playing "house." She worked the pump to inflate the air mattress, which she insisted on for herself, arranged her sheets and blankets and stacked her new clothes on top of her suitcase. They had bought the last two Harry Potters, which Christina hadn't yet read, and when "her room" was arranged she couldn't resist opening the first one and reading before dinner.

"Let's go riding tomorrow. You want to?" Nick asked when they had eaten.

"Aren't we going to wait for Andorra?"

"We can go again when she's here. I know her friend Jimmy, the guy who has the horses. We could ride out to Andorra's house."

"Sure, okay. I'm going to read my book now. Can I take this lamp over by my bed?"

"That's fine. I'll clean up here." By the time he had heated water for dishes, washed them and banked the fire for the night, Christina was asleep. He sat for a long while looking at her and feeling very happy. "Sleep tight," he whispered.

The next morning he rose quickly in the cold room and got the fire roaring again; there was just so much discomfort Christina should be challenged with. The noise of the process woke her. With good grace, she threw on her coat and shoes for a run to the outhouse and came back laughing.

"There was a bird in there! I had to chase it out. Wow, it's cold! Can I have a cup of coffee?"

"When did you start drinking coffee?"

"I don't know. A while ago. I'm nearly fourteen, you know, Dad." Nick smiled as he added more coffee to the drip pot.

Nick and Christina's horses reached the top of the hill where they could look down on Andorra's "Hidden Place." House and outbuildings, workers' pickups and new adobe walls were just visible through the trees.

"This is pretty," she said. "What are those guys building?"

"A bathroom."

"What, actually attached to the house? *There's* a good idea."

They tied the horses where they could reach the runoff from the spring and went over to visit with the crew. Pat showed Nick the newly arrived solar panels, which Al and Lou were mounting on a slanted wooden frame in a good spot for southern sun. The new bathroom contained a utility space for the batteries that would store the electricity generated by the panels. A well crew would start drilling next week.

Christina went off to wander through the house. Nick found her in the kitchen and they went out to sit on the porch. The willow chairs had been moved to the end where the low autumn sun was slanting in under the roof.

"I wouldn't have thought Andorra lived in a place like this. She's like, you know, elegant. Don't you think?"

"Yeah, she is. You know she's lived all over the world. She was born here but she's lived in England and Europe and she just decided to fix up this place. It was her dad's and he's dead now. I'm not sure she knows what she wants to do next, besides writing her book."

"Aren't you going to marry her?" Christina smiled coyly.

"No, Christina. I told you she's not my girlfriend."

"But you guys really like each other."

"Does it look as if we like each other?"

"Dad, are you like clueless? What was she doing down there with you?"

"Well, she speaks Spanish and she wanted to help. She had to go to Mexico for her book anyway, and she was worried about you. She had a situation when she was growing up where her mother took her away

217

from her dad and didn't really pay much attention to being a parent."

"You know Mom uses drugs," Christina said abruptly.

"She always struggled with that, Christina. I hope it wasn't too hard for you. I don't know why she wanted to take you away but I think it will be best if you stay with me and let her get that sorted out."

"Dad, she's not even trying to sort it out."

"She went to rehab, didn't she?"

"That was just because Hal left her and said it was because of the cocaine. She didn't last a week after she got out. She met Chuy and started again. I almost ran away a few times. I hate Chuy."

"He didn't do anything to you, did he?" Nick asked anxiously.

"No, Dad. Don't worry. It wasn't like that. He's just such a creep, *and* a criminal. Sometimes he carries a gun. All Mom wants is his money. She thinks he's stupid and she isn't nice to him." Christina's eyes began to brim with tears. "Oh, Daddy, things were getting worse and worse."

"Come here, sweetheart." Nick pulled her into his lap and held her while she cried. "It's going to be all right," he murmured into her hair, his eyes wet. "I'm never going to let another bad thing happen to you."

On the ride back, Christina took a closer look at the landscape. She exclaimed over the mustard and orange rocks, the reddish winter willows and the intense color of the sky. Nick told her about a local author who speculated that the autumn sky was such a deep blue because it had opened to the infinite coldness of outer space.

"Can you mix in black, like the black of space, with blue to get a color like this?" Christina asked.

"No, pigments don't work that way. It's a challenge to paint light."

"This is what you should paint next." Christina swept her arm to encompass the landscape.

"Maybe we can come out tomorrow and make some studies."

Over the next few days they drove out in the truck with Caran d'Ache pencils and pads of paper. They moved from view to view and Nick pointed out elements of composition and showed her tricks of layering the colors. They talked about the differences in working with colored pencils, water colors, acrylics and oils.

"What are those things up in the sky, Christina?" Nick pointed to some blobs on her drawing.

219

"Those are the spaceships you can just barely see out there in the coldness of outer space."

"I like that!"

On a trip to Santa Fe they visited the galleries on Canyon Road. Christina was especially thrilled with the wild colors some artists used in the Southwestern landscapes—blue hills, red fields, orange trees, purple houses in little villages like Estancia. They ate at a trendy restaurant with casually dressed, elegant people and looked in folk art and jewelry galleries.

"This town's very artsy, isn't it," Christina observed. "I like it. When do we get to your gallery?"

"We're just coming to it. It's that one there." Nick pointed as they strolled up the street.

"Wow, it looks fancy."

"It is. In fact, you're going to be pretty impressed when you see the prices on my paintings."

"Are you selling a lot?" Christina asked when she saw all the zeros.

"Enough."

"Dad, we're rich!"

Nick was greeted warmly by the assistant who discovered them in the room where Nick's paintings were hanging. She was a striking young woman with spiked hair, edgy makeup and a pixy smile. Her fingernails were impeccably done in a blue that matched her silk tee. First cousin to black, Nick thought, but Andorra and her natural, clean, pink fingernails flashed into his mind.

"Nick! I was just about to call you. Joan Winter bought the magenta rock! And who is this? Don't tell me she's your daughter!"

"Yes, this is my girl. Christina, this is Sita. Is Gerard in? I want him to meet her too."

"No, he went to see his sister in Albuquerque. She had surgery. He wanted me to tell you he'll have his packer send your paintings to Berlin. He can come up and get them next week. Should I tell him Monday? You could meet him at the church in Estancia around three and take him to your house. He works with the guy who's making the crates."

"Looks like this is coming together. You're priceless, Sita."

"Always ready to serve." She flashed him a flirtatious look.

Thirteen

The horse picked its way down the switchbacks of the escarpment toward the Cortéz estates south of the capital. The valley below was filled with the delicate green of the sugar cane grown at San Antonio Atlacomulco and at Javier's father's hacienda farther to the west. He skirted the village and factories and rode on into the afternoon, reaching the hacienda as the sun was close to setting. With heavy heart, he rode through the grand portal, dismounted in the interior court and gave his reins to an old Indian servant. Javier knew the man—Pepe; he had once cared for the horses and mules at his parents' house in the city. His mother had been watching for him all day, Pepe said. Javier looked toward the family rooms and caught a glimpse of a shape ducking out of sight behind a shutter—likely his mother. It was not dignified to show oneself at a window even when watching for a beloved son and she had much reason to try to maintain her self-respect in these dark days.

Javier had come to this hacienda frequently over the years—it was one of the estates to which the family retreated when it became too cold in the capital—but he had never liked its cavernous, dark rooms. How painful to think of his mother here for the rest of her days. And to be visiting her secretly for this goodbye, to be part of the pretense that the Sandovals had renounced all Rodriguez de Matos connections following his grandfather's downfall.

When the family had moved house during the social doldrums after the festivities of Navidad, they had traveled with mule-drawn carts loaded with chests of clothing, kitchen equipment and other household goods—even beds, chairs and tables. These remote haciendas were stripped of most of their furniture when they weren't in use; only the heaviest mesquite wardrobes or tables seating dozens—things too heavy to be carried away by thieves—might remain.

His mother had come with her furnishings and bedding, her favorite paintings and decorative objects but they were apparently inadequate for the size of the rooms, and when Javier was led to the *sala,* he found her in barely furnished emptiness. The room, which could have held a hundred guests, contained only two carved chairs, a long table and a sideboard. High windows facing west across the courtyard allowed three narrow rectangles of sunset gilt to slant across the bare stone floor. Javier knew from experience that this brief afternoon illumination was all the room ever received and that the damp never left it. His mother, holding herself as if waiting for her noble guests to present themselves, was seated at the far end.

Javier kissed her, sat in the second chair and took her hand. As he peered into her distracted face, wondering why she did not seem elated to see him, she began to speak as though their conversation had been interrupted only for a moment.

"My darling, more grief than we could have ever dreamed has fallen upon us, and now is added your exile. I don't know how I will bear it but you are young and will no doubt relish the adventure. You have grown the beard of an adventurer, I see." She sighed, looked away, turned toward him again, squeezed his hand. Suddenly animated, she spoke intensely.

"Javi, you must never put your life at risk, you must keep the secrets even in far lands. Hold close the Virgin and see in Her my love. I am certain we may still pray to the Virgin. Do you think She will care for us now that...? Promise me! I have passed to you the blood of God's Chosen. Surely She loves God's Chosen! Find a wife of pure blood, Javi. Never forget your pure blood." Again vacant-eyed, she picked at her sleeve as though she had forgotten that anyone was in the room.

Elena Rodriguez de Matos de la Cruz had believed she was as Catholic a girl as ever lived. When her marriage had been arranged, she had begged to enter the convent instead, and the effort to forgive her parents for refusing her wish had never entirely ended. The archbishop, to whom she had confessed her vocation, had not been pleased either. Her dowry would have bought diamonds to embellish his vestments, haciendas, mines and new palaces—those necessities of the True Church in New Spain. She had always been fragile and had not been trusted with the family secret, until it could no longer be kept from her.

The family suspected that Don Fortunado's downfall had resulted from an accusation by a particular business rival, though the incident with the convent could not have helped, even though it had happened many years earlier.

Elena had collapsed when her mother—who had now entered the convent she had refused her daughter—reluctantly confessed that both her own mother's family, and her father's, had pretended to convert in Spain at the end of the previous century when the other two options had been death or expulsion. The family had reinforced their deception by changing their name from de la Cueva to de la Cruz—"of the Cross."

After her mother's confession, Elena began experiencing visions in which the Virgin explained that it was not the secret Jewish identity, but the family's *abandonment* of their Jewishness that had doomed them, and when she asked an unsuspecting cousin where she could find a synagogue, her husband had felt he had no choice but to hide her away.

Again, she looked wildly into Javier's eyes and grasped his hand in both her own, alarming and frightening him. Was she mad, he wondered? He was tortured by her confused messages: he must be a pure Jew; he must love the Virgin; he must reject Catholicism; he must appear to embrace it for his survival's sake. He tried to calm her, and himself.

"Mother, I am sure the Virgin will keep me safe because you have always loved Her so well. I do promise that I will always honor Her and you."

"More, my child, you must honor your true nature!" She jumped to her feet and crossed the room to the side table where she retrieved a velvet-wrapped bundle. Slowly unwinding the cloth on her lap, she spoke. "Here is a powerful image of the Santo Niño de

227

Atocha. He will bring you food and water on your journey. Javi, it contains holy relics. Holy relics! I must not tell you how I came by them. Never put them from you. For my sake. Remember!"

That night, Javier thought of his poor mother's deranged religious vision, in too many ways like his own. His grandmother had made his path sound clear and simple—if only he could talk to her again—but the Virgin and Her Holy Son! How could you turn your back? How could you pray to "Commandments?" How could you make your living in the wilderness, find your wife, choose your path, without your family to help? He felt more like a child than a man on the cusp of adventure, as his friends insisted on seeing him. They chafed under their fathers' rule and envied him his coming freedom, and he only wished he could change places.

~~~~~~~

The library proved to be packed with treasures. Andorra had found a first-edition copy of the *Historia Verdadera De La Conquista De La Nueva España* by Bernal Diaz del Castillo, one of the company who came with Hernán Cortéz, the conqueror of the Aztecs, and the first Spanish translation of Prescott's *The History of the Conquest of Mexico.* The Prescott book contained an engraving of Gonzalo de Sandoval, one of Cortéz's most trusted lieutenants. Andorra knew that he had died on a return trip to Spain and without heirs—legitimate heirs—but she had always hoped there were misbegotten Sandovals left behind in Mexico who might have passed the name down to her. Gonzalo de Sandoval was reported to have said that he did not believe in God or Divine Providence—clearly a freethinker and brave, too, in those days when the Church could take your life for blasphemy. He seemed like an appealing ancestor.

Each day, Andorra and the old librarian went through their morning ritual of politeness but smiled at each other with genuine affection.

"*Muy buenos días, señorita Sandoval.*"

"*Buenos días, señor Carabajal. ¿Cómo amaneció?*"
How are you this morning?

She had been working for nearly two weeks and they had become accustomed to taking cups of chocolate and *pan dulce,* sweet rolls, in his office each morning as they discussed her progress. Today, however, she rushed through the breakfast, eager to return to the extraordinary contents of the folio she had discovered several days before.

It lay where she'd left it on the table, the greater

229

part of the pages, dense with fine faded script, turned over onto the cover. The title page read: *Historia de la Nueva México* by Gaspar Pérez de Villagrá. What else could it be but the handwritten original of the famous book by the chronicler of the Juan de Oñate expedition published in 1610? Unlike the printed versions in Spanish or English translation with which she was familiar—she even owned a copy—Andorra had discovered that this contained a list at the end (complete, it was claimed) of the expedition members and, for many of them, a description of their exploits, land grants or fates. A gold mine. The sort of discovery historians live for.

Pérez de Villagrá's work, from the days when tales of derring-do were told in verse, recounted the formation of the expedition in Mexico and its thirsty, hungry wanderings seeking the Rio del Norte, now called the Rio Grande. Andorra had long pictured its slow progress with its scouts, wagons, horses and mules; with its seven thousand head of cattle, sheep and goats and its vaqueros, butchers, cooks and blacksmiths; with its families, men at arms, priests, servants and slaves. The company would have covered the landscape and filled the valleys as the expedition carried northward rich traditions: foods such as posole, and songs, among them

"La Llorona" with its origins in pre-Hispanic Mexico and "Las Mañanitas" from the long-past Jewish flowering in Spain. *This is the morning psalm that King David sang...*

The expedition encountered the villages of the Pueblo Indians, some known then by the names they kept today, many not, for designations and most else had changed with the Conquest. All around Estancia, towns founded afterward were called by names of expedition members. Pérez de Villagrá's *Historia* ended with the terrible punitive raid on Acoma Pueblo. He'd announced second volume but it never appeared.

In the listing of the four hundred male expedition members at the end, Andorra had found a name she had never noticed in the body of the book. It was a name that was not likely to have escaped her attention: Javier Sandoval Rodriguez. He had settled on a land grant described as "west of Heishi Pueblo." Andorra's heart had pounded when she saw it. The property of her father, Aaron Sandoval, was west of Heishi.

There was even more to excite her. Some days before, she had found documents from the Holy Office of the Inquisition and had made a copy of every person whose name had appeared in the records in the ten or so years before the expedition had set off. When she compared the two lists, she had seen that a sadly-misnamed Fortunato Rodriguez de Matos was burned at the stake in the little plaza outside this very building sometime in the late 1500s. He had been a *converso* accused of reverting to Jewish worship.

Javier's name, in the Spanish manner, was formed by his father's surname (Sandoval) followed by his mother's surname (Rodriguez). It was the same for women, even after marriage. Thus, Javier's maternal grandfather would have been named Rodriguez. Could the Rodriguez de Matos in the Inquisition records and Javier Sandoval's grandfather have been the same man? Had it been prudent for Javier Sandoval to seek his fortune far away from the shame of his mother's family? And could he have carried an injunction with him to preserve his hidden faith?

Andorra had scanned the pages of the *Historia de la Nueva México* looking for other references to Javier Sandoval. It took two days to reread the text but she found nothing but the familiar self-congratulatory chronicle. Again, God was glorified as the Franciscan friars excused any cruelty in the effort to bring the misguided savages to the Holy Faith, the *Santa Fé*.

Was there any record of family members of persons who had been accused by the Inquisition? This was the question she posed to Señor Carabajal after she had described her discovery. She had told him about the thrill of finding the Sandoval name among those of the expedition members and her speculation about Javier's mother's side of the family. Despite his restrained manner, Señor Carabajal was clearly very excited about her discoveries. He had come to love Andorra's stories about the outpost of New Spain on the upper Rio Grande. He thought about her quest for names of family members for a while and said there was one volume they could consult.

But Andorra's romantic speculation of a connection between New Mexico Sandoval and *converso* Rodriguez de Matos would have to remain just that. The volume Señor Carabajal suggested didn't prove to be helpful. It appeared that her successes in the Pontifical Palace were coming to an end.

She spent the next Sunday beside the hotel pool reading over her notes to be sure she hadn't overlooked anything. Thanksgiving was in less than two weeks. Andorra had talked to Adelina several days before, had been urged to come home for the holiday, and had agreed to do so. If she arrived at the last minute, Nick and Christina would already be in Chicago, so she arranged to fly on Tuesday and be in Estancia on

Wednesday, just in time to help Adelina cook for the crowd of family who would share the day. It was best to reinforce the decision to end her awkward dance with Nick, and she could spend the time until she left Mexico in the nearby town of Taxco, which she had long wanted to see. She would say goodbye to Señor Carabajal and take a bus over for a quiet few days before coming back to Mexico City for the flight home.

Andorra had to congratulate herself on how well she was handling her decision to forget Nick. She was not in the least depressed; she was entirely able to concentrate on her research; she hardly ever thought about their last night or twisted her body in sleeplessness as she relived it. If only there had not been something so eloquent to the way he had moved in her…

Had he thought she would return to New Mexico before he left? Had he quizzed Auntie about her plans? No, he must be occupied with Christina and shipping his paintings. But surely he would have introduced Christina. Why hadn't Auntie mentioned him? She must have seen that they were going nowhere and was being kind.

In a hotel off the little plaza with its gloriously

ornate church, Andorra studied brochures and planned a leisurely inspection of Taxco's sights. Her mind was clear. She was relaxed and had a promising novel to read about art forgery, apparently containing no romance. That was best. The last thing she needed was a tale of true love thwarted, though it turned out she wasn't in need of a tale about a brilliant painter who could imitate the Old Masters, either.

Three days later, with most of her sight-seeing done, she sat on a tiny balcony overlooking the plaza, drinking wine and watching the afternoon sun striking the church's façade at an angle oblique enough for the stone details to preen against their own shadows. She was musing about her research. There had been a Sandoval Rodriguez in the expedition that had left Mexico in the late 1590s, and an executed Rodriguez de Matos, possibly near the same time, but no proof of a family connection between them. The link she had hoped for wasn't established, and likely never would be. No journal of historical research was going to publish information this weak.

Still, it was so tantalizing: the Sandoval name; the location of the grant; the possibility that Javier Sandoval was from a Jewish family in hiding; the possibility that *she* was from a Jewish family so hidden that the concealment had been long forgotten. Back in New Mexico, she could consult the work done on "Jewish" tombstones and check the names of families who had become convinced in one way or another of their Jewishness. Then there would be the search through marriage, death and property records to trace name changes over the generations. Record keeping in New Mexico left much to be desired, she knew. You didn't just go to the church for marriage, baptismal, and burial records dating back to the Magna Carta, as you could in England. It would take time and there would be many dead ends. Not that she didn't love the process and have the house to play with, not that she actually had to return to the UK or get a job any time soon.

She realized she wanted it to be true: being the direct descendant of the family, being, in her blood, part of one of the most convoluted sagas linking the Old and New Worlds. She let loose her imagination. Perhaps Fortunato's wife had gone into a convent to prove her Catholic *bona fides* when he was accused. Perhaps their daughter had been put aside by her panicked husband, and their grandson, the handsome Javier, had ridden off to the end of the earth and had never come back. She could make it into a novel! Javier could build a hacienda in New Mexico. On the site of Estancia? No, at La

Escondida! La Escondida and what had happened there over the centuries would be the focus of the book. She could tell the story in two historical periods: Javier's and her own—how the contemporary Gabriela or Margarita or Isabel Sandoval discovered her links with the past and how it enriched her life. That night, sitting on the bed in the hotel room, she took a stab at the first part of the story.

"A horse walks into a bar. The bartender says, 'Why the long face?'"

"Long face... A horse!" Christina exploded in laughter at her grandfather's joke. The family was sitting at the Thanksgiving table in Nick's parents' spacious third floor apartment on Chicago's Gold Coast. Aunt Marva, Uncle Henry, their son, Jonathan, his wife, Lily, Nick and his parents—all laughed as much in delight over Christina as at the joke. The occasion was perfect with her back in the fold, so grown-up and pretty. They could see that Nick was himself again. They were a happy family.

The joke briefly interrupted a group effort to help Nick and Christina decide where to live. Naturally, the family was pushing Chicago, but Nick said there was no art scene to speak of and they'd have to live far away in the suburbs, to get the right school. Christina's insistence on New York was weakening. It had turned out that her best friend, Clary, had moved to Costa Rica with her family. Other friends didn't seem so important anymore. Nick didn't want to go back and was relieved that Christina was losing interest; anyway, he hadn't found a private school in the city that was accepting pupils for the second half of the term. Somewhere in Europe? No, Nick wanted Christina to try being a normal American girl. Los Angeles? All that traffic. Marva said Philadelphia had been voted a great city to live in. There was lots of culture and wasn't too far from Chicago.

Nick was going to take Christina with him to Berlin for the show. They would spend Christmas there and be home on New Year's Eve. If they had a home and a school, it would be perfect for Christina to start after the holidays. They had about two and a half weeks to figure it out.

"Dad, I know! Let's move to Santa Fe," Christina said with a huge smile.

Nick waited only a moment, nodded. "Okay. Let's do exactly that."

Every limb and branch of the immense, leafless

linden trees on the Unter den Linden were outlined with fairy lights. Four rows of trees marched down the broad avenue, two lining the pedestrian mall in the center, and two more on the other side of the traffic lanes. One seemed to be walking through a magical forest, flowing out from the Brandenburg Gate. It was the day after Christmas.

The show had opened on the 20th at Dieter's gallery on Invalidenstrasse. Presales had already disposed of three of the nine paintings, one to Berlin's Museum für Gegenwart. Amid champagne and hors d'oeuvres, more had been sold and by the end of the evening only two were left.

"You're going to have some tax issues this year, Nick," Dieter laughed, "and so will I."

Dieter had done more than manage the show beautifully, he had made sure Nick and Christina's *Weihnachten* was happy too. They had been honorary family members for the Christmas Eve feasting and drinking, the lighting of the candles on the tree, and the exchanging of gifts. Dieter's family had taken happily to the "English Only" rule and they had all attended a midnight church service where the carols had familiar melodies, if not words.

Also, Dieter had introduced Nick to Annelies. Her

English was a little spotty and she made funny mistakes but thought it was delightful when he laughed at them. No, she didn't have black-painted fingernails, but she wasn't the girl next door, either, and she seemed to have no qualms about offering Nick a good time.

The taxi was easy to find on the Unter den Linden. Nick and Annelies, weaving and holding tight to each other, had just finished a nice meal with lots and lots to drink. They climbed into the cab for the trip to her apartment, during which Annelies took off her panties and tucked them in her purse. Nick was entirely familiar with the uncovered area by the time they arrived and was painfully erect. The cab driver, looking intensely jealous, accepted his money and let them off. They climbed the stairs unsteadily and Annelies squealed with frustration as she searched for her key; they didn't make it three steps into the apartment before they were tearing at each other's clothes.

The sex was too quick. Annelies let Nick know she wanted another round but then turned over and passed out on the floor. After a moment Nick sat up, staggered to his feet and went searching for a bathroom to dispose of the condom. When he returned, Annelies was snoring softly. He sat down heavily on the sofa to collect himself for the trip home. How was he going to get a taxi in a neighborhood like this? He vaguely remembered a nearby thoroughfare. He'd make it back; he'd just have to wait for his head to clear.

Andorra leaned over him, looking furious. She shook a finger in his face. "I told you this would happen if you came here," she scolded. She turned to leave and Nick, now in the middle of a grassy median, started after her. Traffic was so heavy he couldn't cross the street or figure out how she had managed to. He started out again and again but always had to step back. He realized he would never find her.

Annelies snorted him awake and her apartment dimly came into focus around him. He quietly searched out his underwear, pants, shoes and socks, his coat under the pile of her clothes; he never had gotten his shirt off.

Out on the street he walked into the cold wind. It was all too clear now, both his head and the fact that there was a girl stuck in it. The hopeless feeling of loss from the dream was still with him and he tried to turn his thoughts to the pleasure of the recent sex. Wasn't this just the "no strings" he wanted? He was too drunk, that's all; otherwise, it would have been great. He reached the large street and soon a taxi came slowly toward him. See? Everything was fine.

Much *was* fine. After Thanksgiving, Nick and Christina had returned to New Mexico and gone school hunting. Gerard had told him that the Santa Fe Academy would be the best choice and an interview had been set up. Nick had been extremely nervous about Christina's acceptance, though he'd managed to keep her from suspecting his fears. Testing had shown some major gaps in her knowledge, but her IQ was so high and her story so compelling that she was admitted. The school wanted her to start in seventh grade even though she was the age for eighth, while assuring her she could move up in the middle of the year if she performed well; it was a good sign that she was not discouraged and determined to catch up as fast as she could.

The house search had gone well too. They had looked at four or five of Santa Fe's charming adobes and quickly become knowledgeable about walled gardens, corbels, pine or cedar ceiling details, under-the-floor radiant heat and Mexican tile kitchens and bathrooms. They had found a house with lots of charm off Acequia Madre on an unpaved lane. It was affordable, likely because of the smallness of the rooms. The warm brown stucco walls were lined with pink hollyhocks—at least in the summer promise of the real estate photos—and the window frames and garden door were painted periwinkle. The house rambled around three sides of a patio with a living room, kitchen and enough additional rooms for five bedrooms or offices or studios. The kitchen was ample for dining and the living room opened onto a columned portál that ran the length of the east side. The agent said parts of the house were at least a hundred and fifty years old.

Christina settled on two rooms and a bath for herself. The prospect of a bedroom *and* studio was so exciting she was beside herself. Nick divided the rest into his bedroom, his studio and a guestroom/office. In a rush, they had bought beds, a sofa, two chests and some chairs before they left for Berlin.

Tomorrow they would be going back to the U.S. Christina was eager to get serious about life and busy wondering, aloud and endlessly, if she'd make any friends at The Academy, what color she'd paint her rooms and whether having her own television would interfere with school—good, healthy worries rather than ones such as where they'd go if Chuy threw Deborah out. Nick had canceled the cottage in Scotland where he'd planned to stay for the spring and summer and had accepted Christina's advice about working next on a series based on eroded columns and cliffs like the ones he and Christina had seen from Andorra's new road.

Not that he was going up to Estancia in search of Andorra. When she hadn't returned from Mexico, Nick realized she was serious about not having a relationship. He'd made one last trip to the house to deliver the painting; Pat had let him in and he'd left it leaning against a wall. Certainly he had not agreed to move to Santa Fe for any Andorra-related reasons either. It was only coincidence that she would be near this entirely suitable city; it had been Christina's idea after all.

Fourteen

Though it was warm for late February and sun was slanting through the new French doors, the room needed a fire in the wood stove for comfort. Andorra sat at an old pine table with books and papers piled around her computer, working on her novel. The enlarged living room at La Escondida had been replastered and painted warm beige. It was furnished with Chimayo rugs on the pine floorboards, a sofa covered with heavy cotton weave and a picture signed by Nicholson White. Bookshelves covered the wall and entirely surrounded the door to the kitchen, leaving a high shelf for pots, baskets and notable rocks. The shelves were nearly full;

most of her collection had been sent from London, the flat given to new owners along with the cat. La Escondida was home.

Andorra frowned at the computer screen. How to understand the psychology of these *conversos* with their fears, courage and soul-shattering compromises? What did those experiences do to them? She imagined agonized parents whispering in the night, wondering when, or if, to tell the children—children who may have attended convent schools and become thoroughly indoctrinated Catholics. Some parents must have decided to spare subsequent generations the burden of being seen as "Christ-killers" in a world ruled implacably in the name of Christ. But while many *conversos* had eventually truly converted under the pressure of Church and society, some had managed to cling to their Jewishness generation after generation. Andorra wanted Javier's family to be one of these, but with all the confusion a hidden identity would require.

As Andorra's novel opened, Javier's family had been devastated by the Inquisition's arrest and trial of the grandfather. When Fortunado was taken to be "put to the question," or tortured until he answered as the inquisitors wished, the rest of the family had scrambled to save what they could. Their fortunes, their reputations

and their lives were at stake. *At stake...* Andorra realized
the possible relation of the uses with a chill. It was a
foregone conclusion that the grandfather would be "at
stake." The Inquisition's suspicions were never wrong.

The doomed man's wife, Javier's grandmother,
would profess her purity by entering a convent when
she learned her husband had confessed to being a
relapsed Jew. The act would be an attempt to redeem
from suspicion her daughter and grandchildren, her
sisters and their families. The archive in the Pontifical
Palace had provided Andorra with a description of the
investiture of a nun in a Mexican convent in the 1800s.
She would use it in her tale.

Andorra continued the story with Javier's father
arranging for him to leave New Spain with Oñate, giving
him a chance at a new life far away from the stigma that
had marked the family. Javier would say a last goodbye
to his mother in the family hacienda where she had been
hidden after his father had publicly repudiated her and
had the marriage annulled.

Her book proceeded with that play of fact and
fiction she had first envisioned in the Taxco plaza. She
had Javier join Oñate's company in Durango where it
had halted on its way north. His father had to spend ten
thousand gold pesos to buy his place in the expedition,

his steel armor, his horses and to hire his manservant. This would be Bernabé, a wise caretaker on the boy's road to manhood.

Javier received instructions from his father not to return to the capital, even if the endeavor failed, but of course, Oñate did reach New Mexico; the record was clear that the expedition had been in the area around Estancia and Heishi Pueblo in 1598, and there the fictionalized Javier would make his life on the land he was awarded for his participation in the Conquest.

As Andorra thought about his life as a Spanish settler, she puzzled how to make him both true to the historical record and appealing. He would need many laborers to develop his land grant. Would they be from Heishi? Would they be paid or were they slaves? Was there some way to be honest about the history without making her protagonist one of its culprits? A book cover kept forming before her eyes: dark, powerful Javier, his doublet open to his waist, subduing a proud Pueblo maiden. Andorra didn't like it; she had no interest in ripped deerskin bodices.

She knew the first expedition had consisted of both families and young blades like Javier, and when the new territory had proved fertile and the Pueblos apparently easily subdued, more settlers had followed.

By the time of the Pueblo Revolt, just over eighty years later, when the Indians killed four hundred settlers and Franciscan priests and expelled the rest, the Spaniards had increased to over three thousand. Javier's hacienda could have used these settlers for laborers and vaqueros, thereby not being part of the *encomienda* system that had enslaved the indigenous people.

The sound of the cement mixer interrupted her; the guys were back from lunch. With the bathroom and living room finished, Andorra was going ahead with an expansion of the house to the southwest: another room alongside the living room, two more rooms, plus a bath, at right angles to it and a continuation of the porch fronting them. She strolled out to visit with the workers. It was warmer in the sun than it had been in the house and the crew was working in shirtsleeves.

"How's the book going, *prima?*" Pat asked.

"Not as well as your work. I can't seem to get the whole picture. The Spanish settler part has me hung up and I really need to learn more about how they came up from Mexico. I'm thinking Javier will build something like the Martinez Hacienda in Taos: a fortress with family rooms, kitchens, storerooms, blacksmithing, weaving rooms and the like, around inner courtyards. Build it right here, actually, and he'll need lots of workers. I have to figure out his relationship with Heishi Pueblo. The truth is that the settlers exploited the Indians, and worse. Is he doing that or employing them; is their interaction friendly or hostile? Or maybe he's hiring other settlers, like from the village."

"Are you going to use the actual names around here?"

"I go back and forth on that. I changed the name of Estancia and the Oscuro River but 'La Escondida' is so perfect, I really can't think of another name. Do you think I should change the name of the Pueblo? I'm sure they're very proud of their role in the Pueblo Revolt."

"What's the Pueblo Revolt?" Al asked.

"About eighty years after the Spanish came to New Mexico the Pueblos threw them out. They—should I say we?—came back a few years later and re-conquered the Indians; that would have happened after Javier's death. The Pueblos rose up because their holy men were being killed and they were forced to work on the haciendas as slaves, and they also never forgot what Oñate did to them after they killed a dozen Spaniards at Acoma: nearly wiped out the Pueblo and cut one foot off each prisoner, sent the girls to convents in New Spain. I don't know how to write sympathetically about Javier if he was part of all that."

"Maybe he could be like Thomas Jefferson and his slaves. You know, hating the system and trying to be nice to the Indians but like a good man caught in a bad time in history?" Al suggested.

"Hey! That's good, Al. Remind me to check with you when things get tough."

After some more talk, Andorra returned to the house and her book. She pictured a new cover illustration: Javier, doublet neatly buttoned, shaking hands with an Indian while the families of both men looked on in pride on one side and gratitude, or at least temporary tolerance, on the other. And while she was boiling the pot, she could have a scene where the people of Heishi stand weeping in the snow outside the hacienda as Don Javier breathes his last, his family gathered around him. Sometimes even Andorra could tire of the burden of being true to history. Nevertheless, she was yet to create this family, or wife or hacienda. Javier was yet to even see his land. She had work to do.

~~~~~~~

The rain caught Javier and Bernabé in a great bowl of the fragrant blue-green shrub. They stopped and surrendered to the shower since they saw no hope

251

of shelter and the beauty of the place held them. The horses increased the magic by crushing the salvia and releasing an aroma that cleared the head in a most pleasing way. Clouds mounted billow upon billow, purple-black beneath and rimmed above with brilliant pearl and gold. Between the clouds, the sky was a delicate blue. As the shower passed, the older man shook his head in wonderment.

"Truly, Don Javier, this land is a delight for the senses. If we could live off its beauty we would live well indeed."

"We will live well, Bernabé. Of that I am sure, as long as we value manly exertion as part of a good life. That, I think, we will have in plenty." Javier listened to himself playing the part of "leader of men." If only he *were* so sure of himself.

Day after day, he and Bernabé had ridden out from the little settlement along the stream they called Rio de las Truchas, for the trout they never tired of eating. They were exploring the territory Javier had been promised, looking for water and grazing for cattle. The land along the Truchas was perfect for planting if they built acequias—irrigation ditches; the Conquistadors had carried the technique for building them from Andalucía in Spain. Water would be diverted into channels upriver, channels dug to descend at a slope more gradual than the stream, so that the flow would arrive above the rich river bottom, ready to tumble down onto the crops in the fields beneath. Cattle, however, needed the grasses that grew in the hills.

The salvia meadow they had found was beautiful but it was no grazing site; horses and cattle disdained the plant. As the rain eased, Javier and Bernabé searched for an exit from the bowl among the surrounding rocks and eventually found an opening. They could hear water roaring below; apparently they were above the same arroyo they had followed for a time, although then it had been dry.

"There must have been a great storm in the mountains, Don Javier," surmised Bernabé. "Let me go through first to see if there is a path for the horses." He handed his reins to Javier, and despite his shriveled leg, half walked, half jumped down past the boulders. He was back up in a moment. "It's not far to grass these animals will relish. They can manage the trail if we lead them."

When the horses had descended to the pretty meadow, Bernabé tied them and the two men decided to scout the area on foot while the horses cropped the rich grass. Along the arroyo, which already flowing more gently, there appeared to be a passage to higher land and they had followed it only a moderate distance when the vista opened. High grasses filled a large meadow and ascended between the trees that began at its edge. As they crossed the hidden valley, their feet sank into mud, then into water where horsetails grew. A spring was clearly nearby.

"Don Javier, this is a fine place for cattle."

"Yes, they can range in these mountains and water here. We could build a shelter for the vaqueros and corrals and a barn. I can't imagine we will find a finer spot. Let us bring the horses to drink before we return to the camp." Javier clapped Bernabé on the back and smiled with delight.

~~~~~~~

Andorra and her old friend Jessica had nearly finished an expensive lunch at a restaurant around the corner from the Palace of the Governors, the center of Spanish administration in Santa Fe built in Javier's lifetime. The friends had reconnected by running into each other on the street some months before and Jessica insisted that Andorra stay with her whenever she was in town, which she was nearly every week, visiting the Palace archives.

Jessica was the daughter of hippie cabinetmakers Mario and Sushila in Estancia. She had studied architecture, married one of her classmates and now built million-dollar homes in the hills above Santa Fe. All the houses looked like tiered Pueblos rising above the bushy pines, but Santa Fe never tired of those warm curves framed by the bluest of blue skies, even though the winter snows cracked the stucco and the flat roofs were prone to leaks.

Andorra was recounting the meth lab and Acapulco adventures over tea and a shared dessert.

"And then we actually found his daughter in the villa. I went in and chatted up the mother's boyfriend and when I had a chance I whispered to Christina that her dad was outside. There was a guard who kept her from getting away then, but the next day she managed to sneak out and her dad whisked her back to the U.S."

"My God! What a story!" Jessica exclaimed. "Then what happened? Where are they now?"

"We lost touch. I think they went to New York," Andorra said, looking at the plate.

"What happened? You talk like you really liked him. Weren't you attracted to each other?"

"I told him I wasn't interested."

"*Really?*"

"I guess he told me he wasn't interested, either. He wanted to give all his attention to his daughter."

Andorra shrugged. "There are more fish in the sea than ever came out of it—if I get hungry for fish."

"I'm not so sure that's a maxim that still holds," Jessica said. "Anyway, who are you going to find to date up there in Estancia? Everybody's your cousin." She waved permission and Andorra took the last bite of dessert.

"We did have fun though, when we weren't being held at gunpoint. I think I should get back to work. I want to quit early so I can help you get ready for tonight." It was Jessica's husband's birthday.

"Great. I'll get this," Jessica said, pulling the check toward her. "I hope it doesn't take me the rest of the afternoon to find Jim a shirt he'll like."

Andorra made the discovery in the first box she looked at after she returned to the library. As she paged through a collection of real estate transactions dating back to the earliest days of Spanish settlement in Arroyo Hondo County, the name she was searching for finally appeared. One page was so faded she had to study it a long time before she could make out anything about it. But could it be? Yes, perhaps... Yes! "Javier Sandoval Rodriguez," so decorated with flourishes that she followed each letter over and over to be sure. His signature. He had touched this very page. Andorra looked up and tried, unsuccessfully, to calm herself.

When she examined the page again, she noticed that below the name there was more embellished writing or perhaps a drawing. Would that be the name of the other party? No, the orientation was too vertical for a signature and besides the other name was here— Miguel? Velarde Ma...something. The subject of the document appeared to be a sale, but of what and to which of the signatories? She held the page at an angle to see if there were impressions that could help her. There weren't. She looked again at the drawing below Javier's name. It seemed somehow familiar... Andorra sat back in frozen disbelief. It looked like the petroglyph—Frosty the Snowman—from the rock above the spring! Why on earth? Had Javier seen it, adopted it as part of his signature? Here it looked more like three round balls with a slightly curved shape—what she and Papi had called the hat brim—between the top two. Was it possible it was a coat of arms, an escutcheon? It never really had looked as though the Indians had made it. Whatever, the more she examined it, the more certain she was that this was a drawing of the petroglyph. Javier had known La Escondida! It was real.

Could she call it proof of an ancestral

connection? Andorra tried to think of other explanations, tried to work back through everything she knew, but she was too excited to trust her reasoning. Certainly she had found something truly extraordinary. She sat for nearly an hour, her mind racing, then carefully replaced the fragile document in the acid-free box and carried it to the librarian. That was more than enough for one day.

"Did you find what you were looking for?"

"I think maybe I did," Andorra said, her eyes shining.

March passed. The pear tree bloomed and the crab apples too. They rationed their display to every other year so it was special that they decorated and perfumed her first spring at the house. The building proceeded, providing a backdrop of hammering and men's voices in cheerful banter as Andorra wrote day after day.

A cat had recently made herself at home. She liked to sleep in the patch of sunlight at Andorra's feet while she sat at her computer or to join her for a walk. Chosen for her white, russet and gray colors, Andorra's favorites, she fortuitously had all the feline virtues: the love of a lap, a comforting purr and a taste for mice. Of course, she *would* get on the counter but was too graceful to knock anything off. Lloyd's dog had disappeared and was not missed.

Andorra had developed a plan to alternate episodes from the two periods—the history of the Sandovals and the thinly disguised tale of her own exploration of her roots. To enliven the contemporary story, she had decided to use her meth lab and Acapulco adventures—sitting around in libraries and archives, no matter how interesting the discoveries, didn't make exciting story telling. To maintain Nick and Christina's privacy, she had changed names (Ian and Ariadne), details, the location of the events in Mexico, and Nick's occupation.

She still wasn't sure if Isabel (the Andorra character) was the creator of the Sandoval history, consciously using the saga to work out her commitment to the land and interest in her Jewish roots, or if the tale of Javier and his descendants would be presented as true, the view of an omniscient narrator. In any case, the story streams would converge on Isabel, providing her with some near-mystical connection to the earth she called home. She would tie Javier and Isabel together with the discoveries in the Pontifical Palace in Mexico and in the Palace of the Governors in Santa Fe. Perhaps

259

she should have Isabel's father tell her about the family history, his last struggling communication after his strokes.

Andorra accepted that there was much she would never know. The Conquistadors, many of them, came from the sort of families who recorded their genealogies, but their lives of hardship in New Mexico— punishing winters, drought, floods, poor medical care and brief schooling—seemed to have taken away their descendants' compulsion to document their lives. Not that there wouldn't be military, marriage and death records, land transactions and lawsuits. She was only at the beginning of her searches and increasingly intent on following the story faithfully.

Documenting the family's Jewish connection was much more problematic. Crypto-Jews? How could there be records of any of that? She would have to make it up—but why not? There was the historical Rodriguez de Matos, after all, with almost the same name, and following the discovery of the contract and drawing in the Palace of the Governors, she could almost prove that Javier Sandoval Rodriguez had been at La Escondida. Something like what she was imagining *had* happened. She would use an appendix perhaps, with photos of the two images, petroglyph and document, for the reader to compare and, she hoped, be thrilled to know there was some truth to the tale.

Even though many details awaited more research, the writing proceeded smoothly enough for Andorra to feel a heady trust in its progress. It was as if the story were telling itself, as if she could let go and just let her fingers move over the keyboard. Javier was nothing like the overbearing hunk of that first fantasy book cover, rather, he was intelligent and sensitive. He would love the land and describe it in a detail that would mirror Isabel's descriptions four hundred years later; he would excavate the mine—those Spaniards were always looking for gold—and Isabel and Ian would find something precious there too: their attraction to each other. No, Isabel and Ian were not Andorra and Nick. They wouldn't be hopeless at love and commitment. The reader hardly could be expected to put up with the to-and-fro of the real story. Of course, they couldn't just fall for each other immediately—that wasn't acceptable (Andorra had read enough romances to know that)—but they certainly wouldn't part in the end.

Javier had found the meadow and the spring and made the decision to base his cattle enterprise there. Next, he would build a bunkhouse and corrals for branding, winter feeding and for the horses that would help round up the herds from summer grazing in the high country, and start construction of the hacienda. La Vida, the farming community a few miles away—actually Estancia—would prosper too. The villagers would grow grapes for wine, fruit trees, corn, chile, onions and tomatoes and raise animals such as cows, chickens, turkeys, goats and rabbits—but no pigs.

Fifteen

Javier awoke in the simple adobe room before dawn. How could he sleep when he could be reliving the miracle that had occurred, remembering the sweet tones of Inez's voice as she accepted him? "I love you too, Javier. I will be your wife," she had said, so serious and sincere. Her hand had pressed his and she had looked steadily into his eyes. They had made their pact; they had made it between themselves, without consulting her father or her brother. Whom did he have to consult? Bernabé?

Poor Bernabé, Javier had been consulting him without stop for weeks.

"Bernabé, I confess I don't know what to do. Do

I have any hope for marriage with Doña Inez? Does her father know what happened to my family? He is polite to me but I sense a reserve."

"Perhaps, sir, he does not want to lose his daughter. No more reserve than that."

"He would hardly lose her. We live very near. I fear that he feels our efforts on the land have yielded too little to make a proposal from me desirable. Perhaps he wants to save his daughter for a more prosperous hacienda. Perhaps if I could have distinguished myself at Acoma like the great Juan Velarde, or Asencio de Archuleta, even wall-eyed Hernández—"

"I will be forever grateful that you were not nearby to be chosen, sir. It was a bloody business. And the priests ruled it a just war," Bernabé said with contempt. "Pah! 'Just' as your grandfather's murder. And I would have been obliged to be at your side! I fancy neither a war club in my brains nor the killing of women and babes, however savage."

"Still, those warriors have much honor."

"Likely, sir, the decision hangs not on your prowess in arms but on the young lady's feelings. One can see that Don Diego dotes on her, especially since her mother died. And you do have the great advantage of living near his holdings. He may indeed prefer you to all others for that reason alone."

"Bernabé, I fear you are dreaming. How long is

it since I was invited to stay at his home? And he pleaded illness when last I invited him."

Bernabé tried to hide an affectionate exasperation. "He *was* ill! He sent to us for a remedy for his gout! I think your love for Doña Inez keeps you from thinking clearly, if you will forgive me. He invited you less than a fortnight ago, I recall."

When Javier wasn't worrying that Inez, or her father, would never have him, he was agonizing over his mother's insistent but confusing standards and whether Inez met them. Oh, but his mother could not be consulted and Inez was the dearest, most beautiful, most exciting girl in the world. How extraordinary that this pearl was here. And yet, his dear mother without doubt prayed for him daily and hadn't he been safe and more prosperous than he could have hoped, despite his fears that Don Diego might not see him in that light? Did he owe that to her prayers? Did he owe her obedience in this complicated matter of heritage?

Here in the wilderness of New Mexico, the conventions of New Spain were losing their hold. There, he could never have met with Inez without supervision; after they had eyed each other across the theater or politely enquired if the family would be attending the races on the parade ground, their future would have been up to their parents. There, Javier feared, there would have been no future, but a woman here was more a participant in the decisions of her life. Women, even those from notable families like Inez, did not sit gossiping in their *salas*, supposing they had *salas*. They planted kitchen gardens, sewed clothing and washed it; they helped each other give birth and laid out the dead. They even decided whom they would marry.

Perhaps that was why he and she had acted as they had yesterday when they had forgotten fathers, mothers, the Commandments, the Virgin. He had seen only Inez shining before him, eyes bright with love. There, alone together by the Rio de las Truchas, they had acted as though they were the only man and woman left on the earth, or like that first pair in the garden, with no imperative but to seal their pledge with a delirious kiss.

Today was to be the day they would go to her father and ask his blessing. He and Inez's brother would have returned to the homestead from their trip to San Gabriel de los Españoles. No longer avoidable, a crush of fear and guilt held him to his bed. She had to be told. He would always have her precious words to hold close even when she understood about his family and knew that their union could not be. He had received her words under false pretenses; what would she think of him when she knew?

He thought wildly that he should leave this

place this very moment; ride further still into the wilderness; take for wife some savage woman who could never know or care about Christians and Jews. No. He would not have any wife, if he could not have Inez. He would live alone, watch her from afar as she married someone else and had children and… Tears slipped from Javier's eyes and ran down the side of his face. He had no choice but to mount the scaffold like a man. He must ride to La Vida and tell her.

Inez and her black mare appeared from behind the clump of willows on the river bank. She smiled radiantly but the smile faded as she saw Javier's serious expression. "What is it, my love?" she asked anxiously when their horses had drawn together. "You look distressed."

"Doña Inez, thank you for coming. I hardly know where to begin. This is the most painful moment of my life."

"What are you saying, Javier? Why do you address me so formally? Do you no longer wish to marry?"

"No, no, Inez. It is a question of your wishes. Mine are as ever, stronger than ever. My love for you is such that I must risk all, must tell you all. I honor you too much to be silent."

"Javier, you know my wishes! What is this?"

267

Javier drew himself erect but was unable to look in Inez's eyes. "Four years ago, my mother's father, Fortunato Rodriguez de Matos, fell into the hands of the Inquisition and made confession that he was a secret Jew. He was put to death. My family fell into deep disgrace; my grandmother entered a convent and my father put aside my mother. It was to give me a new chance at life that my father placed me with Don Juan de Oñate. Now I find that I cannot accept that gift. I cannot continue to hide all these things, especially from you."

"Javier—"

"No, Inez. There is more. My grandmother told me a thing that I must tell to you. It is true that the families of both my grandfather and grandmother had been among those who had accepted to give up their Jewish faith and become Christian when the choice was put to them in Spain, but they did not give it up. Their blood runs in my veins; it will run in the veins of our children if we marry." He swallowed hard. "I will release you from your pledge."

A breeze with a hint of the coming winter loosed a shower of gilded cottonwood leaves over the two. Javier raised his eyes to Inez and she smiled an intimate smile. "My love, please do not be upset to learn that your story is known, at least among some. It is known to my father and it is known to me."

"Oh, Inez."

"Listen, Javier, you are my delight, but even if it were not so, even if I were not, as I am, ready to follow you all my days, you would still be a most suitable choice. My family left New Spain because of rumors, rumors based in truth, about our ancestry. My father was afraid for us. I am no one to turn my back on you for what you have said. I love my father and will not reject him or his blood, were such a thing possible, nor will I fail to honor the heritage you and I share. I do not know how to accomplish this, but I believe God will assist us and I trust we and our marriage will find favor in his sight."

Javier could not believe his ears. "Inez, Inez, beautiful creature, I am forever at your feet. I never knew a being as lovely as you." He choked with swelling emotion and reached for her, as their horses stood neck to tail, to pull her to him for a kiss. The mare started, rudely interrupting the embrace, but with hands clasped across the distance, they laughed in delight. It had become the most beautiful day of their lives.

"Your little *duenna* knows how much I want you, Inez. She is guarding your virtue until you are mine."

"And she shall have a lash for it, my darling." Inez gave her mare a light tap with the crop. "Come,

269

let's ride to my father's home. I know he will give us his blessing. Come. It's time to join our lives."

~~~~~~~

Andorra created a fine home in the meadow for Javier and Inez. Three children were born, and one died before her parents; Javier would always struggle with the loss of his favorite. She hardly had time to eat, the story gripped her so, but when she turned to Ian and Isabel, the writing bogged down. While their adventures were easy to describe, their personalities and motivations were not. She had to keep them apart until the end to give the story its proper tension, but *what* kept them from just giving up and loving each other? It didn't seem plausible that Isabel wanted to resist the handsome, talented, family-oriented Ian who kept being so kind and reliable and funny. What was Isabel thinking? Andorra tried to avoid the parallel but couldn't: What had she been thinking? And now it was too late to bother to ask.

And Ian? He'd had years to get over his marital mistake. People do eventually forgive themselves for having chosen poorly. You could even say his daughter needed a mother—a brother or sister too. Why did he think he had to choose between her and new love?

Andorra decided to put off thinking about the problem. It had been several days since she'd last seen Adelina. She would drive in to Estancia.

The afternoon was spent making tamales and recounting the new parts of Javier's story. Adelina was extremely interested in the family being crypto-Jews, though she had no knowledge on that subject to add. Her parents had never talked of anything like that and she was sure they had been believing Catholics. They always made the pilgrimage to the Santuario de Chimayo, until they got too old, though they hadn't gone much to mass. That was likely because they were in the faction of the town that had disapproved of the priest, Father Benedict, because he lived with two women—for a while, three. I should write about the history of this town next, Andorra said to herself, smiling. Write and take cover. Here, as Faulkner had quipped about the South, the past wasn't even past.

Adelina wondered if Javier and Inez would have had a house in town. Could it have been the ruin next to the old convent? I'll see if I can fit that in, Andorra told her. She hadn't yet mentioned that the book would also be about Isabel and Ian. Adelina was sure to draw embarrassing conclusions when she heard, and Andorra wanted to avoid one of her piercing looks as long as possible.

It was early evening when Andorra started back home with warm tamales wrapped in foil beside her on the seat. As she passed the grove of cottonwoods on the road to the house, she slowed down as she saw someone walking ahead of her. When she was near, the person turned around and stood still. It was a young girl. *It was Christina.*

Andorra slammed on the brakes, stared in amazement and jumped out of the truck to take her in her arms.

"Christina! I can't believe it. How are you? What are you doing here? I'm so glad to see you!"

"I'm so glad to see you too! I hoped you'd be here," Christina laughed with relief.

"Where did you come from? Where's your dad?"

Christina looked at the ground. "Don't be mad. I ran away from home."

"Ran away from home! Where is home?"

"Santa Fe. I took the bus from Santa Fe."

"Santa Fe! You live in Santa Fe? I can't believe it. I thought you were in New York. Oh my goodness. Get in the truck. We'll go home and talk this out."

Over a dinner of tamales and salad, Andorra

heard the long list of Christina's grievances: Nick wouldn't let her have her own TV; he had banned video games on school nights; her teachers were horrible; she'd gotten a terrible grade in math; and her boyfriend was grounded because his parents found pot in his bedroom. No, she didn't smoke pot—well, hardly ever. There had been a great party and her dad hadn't let her go just because there was going to be a keg of beer.

Andorra found herself completely delighted to see Christina and to be the person she trusted for help. It was hard to put on a serious face she was so happy.

"Christina, I can see things are pretty rough. I'm glad for you to stay but you know I'm going to have to call your dad tonight."

"No, don't call him! Well, maybe tomorrow. He'll probably come up and drag me back."

"I'll ask him not to do that but I have to tell him you're safe. You know he'll be calling the police and be terribly worried. You don't really want him to worry, do you?"

"I don't care. He's all over me. I can't do anything I want. It's like he doesn't trust me and won't let me grow up."

"Okay. Looks like you and your dad need a break but I know for a fact, Christina, that he loves you totally.

I'm sure we can solve these problems if we work on it. Now why don't you take a hot bath and curl up in my bed—I'm afraid I don't have a TV either—and I'll go up the road so I can get a signal and tell your dad you're all right. Then we can talk some more. Let me put in the number. And don't get any ideas because I'm calling him. There are bears out there."

"Don't worry, Andorra. I've walked enough for one day."

Andorra took the truck to the top of the ridge not far from Estancia, feeling hot and cold all at once. Without knowing what she was going to say, she found the number in the cell's phone book and pushed the call button.

Immediately there was a frantic "Hello?"

"Nick, it's Andorra. I've got her."

"Andorra! Thank goodness! How is she?"

"Absolutely fine. Rather delighted to have an audience for her gripes. She ate a big dinner and at the moment she's in the bath."

"I was so afraid she'd been kidnapped again, I'm almost relieved she ran away. I guess she was afraid to come back after she snuck out to that party last night."

"The one with the keg?"

"Yeah."

"Ah, she neglected to tell me she went to the party after all."

"Andorra, what should I do? I'm off the deep end."

"A time-out's not a bad idea. Can she stay up here? Does she have to get right back to school?"

"No, it's spring break."

"Great. I'll call you tomorrow and let you know how we're doing. I'll try to get a message through the hormone barrier."

"I'll let the police know. Christ. I wasn't ready for all this. I thought we were doing so well. I guess it's not unusual?"

Andorra laughed. "No, Nick, unusual it's not. Listen, I want to get back. I actually have to drive down the road to make a call so you can't reach me but I promise I'll keep in touch. I'll talk to you tomorrow, okay?"

"You've lost your accent."

"Oh, have I? I suppose I really must stay over here then. You can't imagine how unmerciful the Brits are when they think one of their own has gone native."

Nick's laugh had a note of giddy relief. "Okay. A million thanks, Andorra. Good night."

"What did Dad say?" Christina asked as she crawled into the bed.

"Thank goodness."

"Anything else?"

"He said you have spring break and you can stay up here for a while if you want."

"Just like that?"

"No, I asked him if you could stay. He's very worried but wants you to have some space if you need it. It's not like he doesn't want you back."

"Yeah, right."

"He knows you're safe up here. Are you tired?"

"Yeah. I think I'll go to sleep. Can I stay in your bed?"

"Sure. Sleep tight. I'll come in a little while. Do cats bother you? She likes to sleep in the bed."

"No, I like cats. Good night."

"Let me give you a kiss," Andorra said, bending over Christina with a smile. After she kissed Christina's forehead, Andorra touched her fingers to her lips and slid her hand under the pillow. "And here's one for later," she whispered. It was the way Papi had put her to bed.

As she washed the dishes and straightened the kitchen, Andorra thought about Christina's impulsive escape. How fortunate she'd found her; what would the child have done if she hadn't come home? She shuddered, then smiled and chuckled. Poor Nick. Christina was leading him a merry chase.

Sixteen

The next morning Christina seemed sad. She was quiet at breakfast and went out to sit on the porch alone. Andorra went out to her.

"Come on, Christina. Let's go for a walk. I want to show you a beautiful place."

Andorra and Christina crossed the meadow, hiked down the arroyo and eventually climbed up to the sage bowl. The morning air was crisp but the sun was already hot. They stripped off jackets as they went and tied them around their waists.

"I want to show you my rock," Andorra said, leading the way through the sage. "Up you go. This is where I used to lie all by myself when I was just a little older than you and think about my problems."

"What problems did you have?"

"I had mother problems—not dad problems—but big mother problems. My mother left my father and took me away with her. I finally was able to come and visit him in the summers but I had to live with her the rest of the year. She was rather crazy and I felt like I had to grow up too fast with her. Of course, I wanted to grow up fast but things would get out of control."

"Like what?"

"I started drinking early. She thought that was fine. She even thought it was funny if I got drunk, but it wasn't funny and I got myself into some situations I didn't see coming."

"My mom's like that too. She lets me drink. My dad is like through the roof if he thinks I'm drinking."

"Have you talked to your mom?"

"Dad said we should call her to tell her we were in Santa Fe, but her phone didn't work."

"Did that make you sad?"

"No. A little."

Andorra sighed and lay back on the rock with her eyes closed and Christina stretched out beside her.

"Why do you think your dad doesn't want you to

drink?"

"General principles, I guess."

"I think I know why, Christina. Grown ups are usually afraid to tell kids what they're scared will happen for fear they'll give the kids ideas and cause those things to happen."

"I don't think my dad wants to talk to me about sex."

"Do you think sex and drinking are related?"

"Yeah."

"I suspect your dad is afraid of what happens when you, and everybody else, drinks. Inhibitions go out the window. Normally, you don't see a cute guy and just go over and sit on his lap. You don't get in a car with a drunk driver and you don't let someone you hardly know put his hand between your legs. You are stopped from doing that by your right mind. If you drink you aren't in your right mind and you aren't stopped."

"I guess." Christina turned her head away.

"Boys will happily believe that anything is all right to do if the girl isn't calling a halt. Usually the problem is with older boys who aren't as shy as the boys in your class."

"I guess. My friend Lisa got drunk and had sex with a friend of her brother's. She said she doesn't really remember it. Now whenever he comes over she hides in her room. What am I going to do? Everybody in my class drinks."

"It's really tough when everybody's doing it. You could say you can't drink because you're on antibiotics, or you could pour your drink out when nobody's looking. You'll grow up soon enough and alcohol won't affect you as much as it does now. You'll be able to drink without doing anything too foolish. It's impossible to understand that when you're a teenager and your brain isn't mature. Adults look back and say, 'What was I thinking?' So your dad has to keep warning you. Me too."

"If I told my dad about Lisa, he'd about fall down dead or he'd tell Lisa's mom and dad! He's so totally like nervous all the time. I can't stand it."

"Yes, it would scare him because he'd think how he'd feel if it were you. But he'd want to know and he'd want to love you twice as much. He probably would want to tell Lisa's mom and dad, and it *might* be the best thing for her, if they love her like your dad loves you. But that's best left to Lisa." Andorra had a sinking feeling. Was Christina really talking about Lisa? She sat up. "Look, there's a Red-tailed Hawk."

"Where?"

"There, see? Beautiful. Let's go back and have lunch."

"Did you find a nice house in Santa Fe?" Andorra asked as she made sandwiches.

"Oh, yeah. I have a bedroom and my own living room and studio."

"Do you have a living room *and* a studio?"

"No, they're one room, but my bedroom is separate."

"Wow. It must be enormous. How many rooms are there?"

"Let's see. Dad's bedroom, his studio, the guest room and office, my two rooms, and the living room and kitchen. That's seven and two bathrooms." Christina counted on her fingers.

"You two must be rattling around in there." Hidden agenda: Is it just you two? Andorra hadn't been able to control her curiosity.

"The rooms aren't very big. It's a real old house like this one."

"Is your dad glad he moved to Santa Fe?"

"Sure. I think so."

"Has he found friends?" This was embarrassing.

"He's friends with Gerard from his gallery. Some

artists too. Mostly he keeps an eye on me. It's driving me nuts."

"Christina, I've been meaning to ask you if you would read some of my book and tell me what you think," Andorra asked that evening.

"Yeah, sure. Is this the book you were working on in Mexico?"

"In a way. It's about New Mexico; how this land—exactly here—was settled by the Spanish over four hundred years ago. I think this is the latest draft. Yes, this is it." Andorra handed Christina some pages that contained none of the Ian and Isabel material. "I'd appreciate it if you'd tell me if you come across references that you don't understand and especially if it interests you and makes you want to read on. I thought I'd go out and give your dad a call. Would you like to talk to him?"

"No. I know he's being nice to you but he'd really be mad at me. I'll stay here."

"Sure. Here's a pencil. Mark it up. Just like your English teacher."

"I wouldn't be that mean."

"Hi, Nick. It's me."

"Hi, counselor. How's it going?"

"She's at home reading my book."

"What? Your history of the Conquistadors and the crypto-Jews?"

"It got a little more user-friendly. I decided to write a novel. My research has had some great successes but the gaps are too wide for a scholarly work so I'm taking the imaginative route. I can talk your head off about it; I have a totally one-track mind, but at the moment we have Christina."

"What do you think?"

"I don't know yet. She's been talking about her life. I'm wondering if her problems with you aren't actually the central focus of her concerns."

"What do you think they are?"

"Let me give it some more time. I think she'll open up."

"Do you think I should set up some family counseling for the two of us? Do you think that could work?"

"I suppose it depends on the counselor. I'd say it should be a woman and definitely someone Christina says she likes."

"What do you think I'm doing wrong?"

"Well, Nick, I haven't heard much about your life

except that you can be a beast about television and chat rooms."

"Did she tell you about the boy she was romancing on Facebook?"

"How did you find out about that?"

"Jesus. I hate to admit it. I saw her page when she was out of the room."

"I know you can't take chances with what happens online. What were they saying?"

"It was just sweet stuff but what if he's actually the pervert around the corner? It's not like when we were young."

"When I was young, my mother and I were sailing the Mediterranean with creepy Greeks. There were perverts in the next stateroom."

"What? Were you—?"

"No, no. I know it's a real terror being a parent today."

"Uh, how are you doing?"

"I'm fine. The writing has really grabbed me and I have more building going on too. I'm adding several rooms and another bath and I'm going to do a lot of planting in a few weeks. How did you end up in Santa Fe?"

"It was Christina's idea. I was so glad she gave up

on New York. I'd had my fill of the art scene there. I like it here. We found a nice house near Acequia Madre. I thought things were going great, until recently when Christina started flipping out."

"Are you painting?"

"I was. I'm kind of bogged down at the moment. Andorra, uh, I'm sorry I haven't been in touch. I didn't know—"

"That's fine. Don't mention it. I guess I'll go. I'll check in again tomorrow. Maybe I can bore her out of her mind in the country and she'll demand to be returned to you."

As she drove back to the house, Andorra did think about how Nick had been a little more than an hour away for months and had never tried to contact her. She remembered the night in Mexico—it appeared neither of them could hold their alcohol either. Inhibition out the window, just as she'd told Christina. Now the barriers were up and she was sad.

"Andorra can I talk to you about something?" Christina sat on the porch floor with her legs swinging over the edge. Andorra was in one of the willow chairs. Here it comes, she thought.

"Sure."

Christina didn't say anything for a while. "Where do these pieces of pottery come from?"

"From right here around the house. You'll see them sticking out of the ground after a rain. I've been collecting them since I was a child. They have a museum over at Heishi Pueblo and these have the same designs as their pots. I've always wondered how so many came to be here." Andorra stopped talking and waited.

Christina moved the shards into a circle. "You can't tell my dad."

"There might be things he'd need to know. Are you going to tell me something like that?"

"I don't think so."

"Okay."

"Something really bad happened at a party and I guess it was like you said. I was drunk."

Andorra felt a chill. "Yes?"

"I went out in a car with this boy and he got his thing out and wanted me to rub it with my hand and I did and then I felt like I was going to be sick and I got out of the car and threw up right by the door. He was like 'Eyew, that's disgusting,' and then I found out he told a bunch of people."

"Aw, baby. That's too bad. What an awful thing

to happen." And what a relief if that was all.

"You won't tell my dad?"

"No, I don't think he needs to know that." They sat in silence for a while. Andorra sighed. "You know, you don't have to do it again. I mean, if he asked you, or somebody else did. You don't have to do anything you don't want to do, even though sometimes boys try to make girls think they're supposed to. It seems to me that the boys who try to get young girls to do sexual things aren't exactly the nicest people. That guy was terrible— making fun of you for getting sick and then talking about it. Sometimes I think you feel worse for having anything to do with a person like that than for the sex part."

"Yeah, I'm really embarrassed and I'm afraid this boy I like will find out."

"Boys lie about sex all the time. I think it would be fine if you just pretended it never happened. If some boy says, 'Do that with me because I heard you did it with him,' you could say, 'What are you talking about?' Or if you liked him, you could say, 'I like you but I don't want to do that.' And if he says, 'Why not?' all you have to say is, 'I just don't.' If he heard something, he'll think it mustn't have been true. Believe me, Christina, a boy who really likes you is not going to stop liking you because you won't do those things. That never happens."

"But I think boys do like girls who do stuff like that."

"They certainly like to have those things done to them, and it's not *evil* to touch a boy's penis or to get excited and want to be sexual. It is, however, a very bad idea to have sexual intercourse. You do know what I mean, where a boy puts his penis in your vagina and ejaculates?"

"Of course I do."

"I thought you did. It's a bad idea even if you use a condom or he says he'll pull out. If you got pregnant at your age it would be terribly sad."

"I know."

"Here's a true thing. It hardly ever happens unless you drink too much."

Christina shyly showed Andorra the book pages she had read. "I thought it was really good. I didn't know anything about the Inquisition. I put some question marks where I didn't understand things, like why was it so bad to be Jewish?"

"Hmm, good question. Christians decided quite early on that Jews were guilty of killing Jesus and set about killing and persecuting them. They thought it was especially evil for Jews not to accept Jesus as their Messiah since he had been one of them."

"What's a Messiah?"

"Oh, dear. I think the Jewish Messiah was like a king who would come and rule perfectly but, for Christians, Jesus was the Messiah and he died to save them from their sins. Has anyone ever taught you about religion?"

"Chuy was like totally horrified that my mom didn't care about religion, but she doesn't. My dad says if I want to go to church, I can. Do you go to church?"

"No. Neither of my parents were religious and I'm not either."

"Chuy took us to the shrine of the Virgin of Guadalupe in Mexico City. You should have seen! People were like walking on their knees and crying. *He* was crying. He bought about thirty rosaries and coffee cups and pictures that switch from Jesus to the Virgin when you turn them and stuff to hang on the rear-view mirror. Was it the Virgin of Guadalupe that Javier's mother was talking about?"

"It could have been. The Virgin appeared to Juan Diego—you know the story?"

"I guess! Chuy made sure of that and I saw the picture on the cloth."

"She appeared in the 1530s and my story starts in the 1590s. I'm not sure if she was as popular with the upper classes as she was with the Indians, though." Andorra turned more pages of the manuscript. "Let's see, you didn't understand this part about what Javier's mother said to him?"

"I couldn't figure out if she was being Catholic or Jewish. Like she's talking about the Virgin and that's Catholic, right? Then she's talking about the pure blood and that seemed like she wanted him to be Jewish. Then she gives him holy relics in a statue and that seemed Catholic."

"I was trying to make her crazy, as if she had fallen apart because she didn't know what she was anymore. Javier says she's mad, doesn't he?"

"Yeah. I guess it's good the way you show it. I think I kinda got it. No, I got it."

Christina had been at the house for four days and it had been time to deliver her washing to Adelina; she was wearing Andorra's jeans and T-shirt as they drove back to La Escondida. Andorra proposed a plan.

"What do you say we invite your father up for a conference? Are you beginning to think of going back home?"

"You'd help us talk about our problems?" Christina looked anxious.

"If you want."

"You don't think he's still mad at me?"

"I don't think he ever really was but I imagine he sounded pretty angry sometimes. He's probably scared he's doing a bad job of raising you, that if he shows you he isn't sure what to do, you'll lose confidence in him. Something like that."

"Okay, let's invite him up. We could eat the rest of those tamales."

"Hi, Nick. Checking in." Andorra talked in the truck while Christina wandered around outside.

"How's it going?"

"We want to invite you up for a visit. I think Christina's missing her friends, and you. The plan is to have a conference about your issues. I think if she sees you aren't upset with her, she'll probably want to go home. I'm supposed to mediate. Perhaps I can actually help, but you can tell me if I'm out of line."

"I can't imagine you out of line."

"Oh, it could happen."

"Do you have ideas about what's been bothering her?"

"I have some confidences, but it's all normal growing-up stuff. It really takes me back. She's a good girl. The critical thing is for her to trust that you're going to love her, stand by her, help her make good decisions. I'll make sure she knows that I'm always ready to listen."

"When shall I come?"

"Tomorrow morning?"

Seventeen

Andorra smiled as she watched Christina pace the porch and peer up the driveway each time she reached the end. She glanced at the list of topics for the conference waiting on the kitchen table. As they had talked things over the previous night, the list had been rewritten twice as Christina had capitulated unbidden on various points of contention. First, her demand to be allowed to play video games on school nights had been rescinded.

"What about the TV? What do you watch?" Andorra had asked.

"I watch *Survivor* and some *Big Brother.* I can

only watch it when Dad is out or in his studio. I saw a few episodes of *Big Brother* with him but he thought the people were dumb."

"So he doesn't want you to have a TV in your room."

"He said we could talk about it if my grades came up."

"What about your maths? Do you think you should be studying more?"

"What do you mean, 'maths?'"

"We say 'maths' in England. Sorry."

"I think one is enough."

"Ha! Point taken."

"I'm really stupid in math."

"I doubt that. I can see you're very smart. You just weren't taught the basics. Have you ever thought of getting a tutor?"

"Dad said I could have one. I guess I could try it."

"Why not? It's not your fault that you jumped around from school to school. My mother never kept me in one school long enough for me to learn anything."

"Okay. I'll say I'd like to have a tutor."

"I'm sure that will help. And your dad's going to want to talk about drinking and keg parties and such."

"I'll try to do better. I don't much want to go, I

guess. I mean, I do and I don't."

"You are rather underage, you know. The police could even show up."

"I heard that happened with some kids at the school last year."

"What happened to them?"

"I'm not sure but I heard there were like assemblies every week. It was a big deal."

"So the police are on the case."

"I guess so. Maybe I could get my boyfriend to come over and visit when there's a party and we could have fun and stay out of trouble."

"What does he think about drinking?"

"He's in total pot trouble at the moment. Maybe he couldn't even come over. He's majorly grounded."

"Perhaps your dad could talk to his parents."

"Maybe."

This girl was all right, Andorra had thought. Nick was probably getting himself ready to compromise on points Christina had already abandoned.

At last he drove into the yard and Christina ran out to hug him—a good start. They put their arms around each other as they walked up to the house; Andorra waited on the porch. She and Nick exchanged a social hug and kiss. She remembered his smell. In the house, Nick approved the living room, bedroom and bath, thanked Andorra for hanging his picture, accepted coffee, sounded nervous. He and Christina sat on the sofa and Andorra turned her desk chair to face them. The cat, fickle beast, curled up in Christina's lap. Nick tried not to notice what a knockout Andorra was.

"So, Christina, we're going to talk about our problems?"

"Right, Dad. I made a list of the stuff we were fighting about."

"Pretty organized, sweetie. Okay, let's hear it."

"Number 1. Grades."

"Well, just math."

"Dad, math is hard for me and Mr. Richardson explains things too fast."

"We knew that would be a problem when you took your placement tests. We haven't been working very well together on that, have we. What have you been thinking?"

"You told me I could have a tutor and I said that wouldn't help, but now I think maybe I'd better give it a try."

"Good. We'll get a tutor. Does your friend— Daisy? Does she like the one she has?"

"Yeah, but her grades haven't gotten better. The

school is always saying they have a list of tutors."

"Okay, I'll call."

"Right. Number 2. TV In My Bedroom."

"I still don't know."

"That's okay, Dad. I can watch TV in the living room. There's nothing much on, anyway. Number 3. Computer On School Nights. What if my math grade came up? Can I do Facebook?"

"What are we going to call up?

"B?"

"Fair enough. But how about Facebook only on the weekend."

"Dad!" Christina elaborated it into multiple syllables. "If I don't upgrade my page, pretty soon nobody will look at it!"

"Christina, I have the impression that Facebook needs to be upgraded about every thirty seconds. If you get six kids online going back and forth, I don't see how you can get any homework done, any of you."

"It's the age of social networking, Dad!"

Nick gave a terse laugh. "Tell me about it. Look, I really want you to do your homework first. Then... Christina, I worry that too much of that stuff is gossip that can get out of hand, even be cruel. Are you sure that's the best use of your time? You talk to everybody in school every day. Shouldn't you be reading books?"

"Oh, Dad. You know I read lots of books. You just hate Facebook. And you have a web page."

"That's what artists do. It's different. It's just for helping buyers find me."

"Let's see," Andorra said. "It seems to me that Nick is worried about bad things that can happen online and Christina wants to take part in the good things. Right? If your dad lets you network with your friends, Christina, can you promise to go to him if things get weird, even if it's embarrassing? He has to know you won't be in danger, that you'll never have anything to do with a stranger online, especially agreeing to a face-to-face meeting."

"Okay. I see. I'd never do that. I promise."

"So we're going to have a computer moratorium on weekdays, look for a tutor to help you get up to a B in math and have a homework-first rule," Nick summarized.

"Right." Christina sighed.

"It will go fast, Christina. I'm sure you can get a B on your next report if you work hard."

"Dad, you have too high standards for me!"

"Christina, I've known you all your life. I know how smart you are. You read at college level! I know you can do it."

"Okay. Okay. We've got one more. Number 4. Drinking Parties. I've decided I'll say you won't let me go because sometimes the police come."

"That's great, baby, but we have to find a way for you to have fun with your friends, like going to movies or having kids over."

"I thought of that too. That'll be good. Everybody thinks it's cool that I have my own living room."

"I have one big request, Christina. I want you to promise never to run away again. I've never been so scared in my life."

"I'm sorry, Dad. I promise."

"Give me a hug on it, baby." The cat escaped with an insulted yowl.

"I think I should start lunch," Andorra said. "I'm feeling pretty useless around here."

"That is really incredible that you have the petroglyph drawing on a document. I can't get my head around it. By the way, does your book have any buried Spanish gold?" Nick asked. They sat at the blue table in the kitchen eating tamales.

"Not yet. There is a gold mine, though. You know the old mine." Andorra looked away. Why did she mention that?

Nick cleared his throat. "Do you know why I say that about buried gold?"

"You like clichés?"

He laughed. "No, it's because there's something I can't get out of my mind. When we buried your father's ashes, we thought the shovel struck a rock, but there was something wrong about it. The sound? The hardness? Something. You were thinking about your father and I didn't want to say anything, but every now and again I remember it. I thought about it a lot while I was doing the painting, and now you tell me how important the petroglyph was to Javier, and I'm wondering if something wasn't already buried there."

"Really? What an idea." Andorra frowned and put a hand to her mouth. She thought for a long moment. "Let's go see! I don't think Papi would mind. We'll take him on one last adventure."

They left the dishes on the table and headed first to the barn, where Andorra picked up a shovel and trowel, and then on to the rock, while Christina bounced with excitement.

There was no sign that the earth had ever been disturbed. The grass had started its spring growth, lifting last year's aspen leaves with velvety insistence. Nick and

Andorra consulted on where to dig; he removed a section of turf and laid it aside as he had before. Before long the shovel hit the box of ashes. Andorra knelt, scooped the earth off it with her hands and lifted it out.

"Hi, Papi," she said. "The box is doing fine, isn't it?"

Nick poked at the bottom of the hole with the trowel. Almost immediately there was a scraping sound—definitely not trowel on rock. "Wow. There is something here," he said softly, looking at Andorra. With great care, he scooped away the earth. Something that looked like heavily pitted and corroded metal began to appear. Its dimensions apparently extended beyond the edge of the hole on one side—how nearly they had missed it when they dug in September—and he slowly enlarged the opening.

"My turn," Andorra said excitedly. "I think we should try to get it out with the earth packed around it. It could be very fragile." She took the trowel and started down one side a few inches away from an edge. "We'll have to dig under at some point. These sides are at right angles; it may be another box." She started on a second side.

After Nick had taken another turn, a free-standing rectangle rose from the bottom of the hole. He sat back and worked his shoulders. Digging so far below the surface was awkward. "Any ideas about how we're going to get under it?"

"The hole's still not big enough. We'll have to enlarge it again so we can come at it from the side. Let's make it big enough to put the smallest person down there to dig."

"That's me!" Christina crowed.

"Why, I think you're right," Andorra said, as though marveling that she hadn't realized that before. She smiled and winked at Nick.

While Christina went to the house for a kitchen knife and drinking water, Nick dug at the sides of the hole, and when she came back, it was ready for her to climb in. Crouching beside the object in its earth crust, she removed dirt from beneath it—seriously, carefully, slowly—until it was loose and could be dragged atop a piece of 1x12 from the building scraps. A length of rope from the barn was looped around it and, with Christina's steadying hand, Nick and Andorra lifted the heavy lump to the surface.

"This is heavy enough to be gold," Andorra exclaimed as they carried it to the house. "But don't you two think you're getting any. It's on my land."

"You never would have known about it if it

wasn't for me," Nick insisted, mock indignant.

"I was the one who got it loose," whined Christina, catching on to the game.

"One *escudo* for each of you and that's it." When they reached the house, Christina rapidly cleared the dishes from the table; they set the object in the center and stood back looking at it.

"First let's put Papi back in the earth and then see what we have," Andorra said.

As the rosewood box was replaced in its now-deeper grave, Andorra whispered, "I promise, Papi, no more disturbances. I'll let you know what was keeping you company down there." Nick shoveled in the earth, Christina and Andorra pressed it down, and the three went back to the kitchen for the inspection.

Andorra had the idea to drip a tiny bit of water over the dirt so that it would come loose more easily. She picked cautiously with a paring knife, and had nearly uncovered the rotted wood and metal scrollwork on one side, when it and part of the top collapsed. She pulled back in horror and then leaned in for a closer look. Hinges and a corroded lock could be seen; the thing *was* a chest and they could see lumpy cloth in the interior.

"Doesn't seem to be gold," Andorra said, "but this is old, very old. As she tugged gently at the wrapping, the cloth partially fell away from a complex metal shape. She teased more and more of the material free.

"What *is* this thing? Does this look like a candle holder? And another one? A little candelabra? Oh my God, this could be...oh, it is! It's a menorah! Look. One, two, three, four, five, six, seven, eight, nine. It's all here. Oh, heaven help me, we've found Javier's mother's holy relics."

"What are you talking about?" Nick asked.

"It's my story! It's as though it were all true!" Andorra cried.

"What's a menorah? Somebody tell me!" yelled Christina.

"Whew. Right. I've got to catch my breath. A menorah is a candelabra used to celebrate Hanukkah. That's a Jewish holiday. Jerusalem was under siege and the Jews couldn't get oil for the temple lamp but the lamp miraculously burned for eight days anyway, so Jews light a candle for each of the eight nights. This has holders for the eight candles and the ninth is for the candle that lights the others. This is exactly what menorahs look like."

"This is incredible," Nick said.

"I'm going to have to take this to the museum. Look, there's more stuff in here but I don't think we dare do any more. Maybe they can tell what period the box and the menorah are from and what this material is. I think I badly need a cup of tea. How about you two?"

As they sipped their tea, Christina exuberantly told Nick about the Inquisition, the convent and Javier's mother's holy relics, delighting in her expertise, and Andorra took off on new story lines that would include the box. In the midst, she paused.

"Over and over, after his strokes, my father tried to tell me something. All I could make out was that it was about the rock and the petroglyph. I thought he was telling me where to bury him, but now I wonder if he knew something about this, about the family. Perhaps he wanted to tell me, but waited too long. I wish I could know!"

The shadows were lengthening. Christina had announced that she would go back with Nick; they could stop by Adelina's for her clean clothes on the way. Nick promised they would visit and return Andorra's things soon, but she said she'd take the box to Santa Fe in the morning and could drop by the house to pick them up. Christina groaned that she would have to clean her rooms. Before they left, Nick helped Andorra put the box into a cardboard carton that they then placed on the front seat of her truck with a seat belt securing it. It was late afternoon when they drove away.

Andorra sat on the porch and watched the sunlight slant over the meadow. The events of the day were too remarkable for thought; it was as though a warm comforter of blessing had settled around her. She was so glad that Christina had come to her, and had gone with her burdens lifted. Papi felt very near; she was filled with gratitude for all he had given her. How poignant it was that he had died without learning about the chest, and yet, that it was his death that made possible the discovery linking the family to a tradition that stretched back twenty generations. The land was giving up its secrets as though it had waited for her to be born. She put her head on her knees and cried with an overflow of emotion she couldn't name.

Andorra drove to town early the next morning. She knew one of the museum's curators, and as soon as she reached the ridge, she called to see if he was in. Henry said he'd be thrilled to see her, and the menorah. Drive carefully, he admonished excitedly.

At the museum, she went down to the basement laboratory and found a helper to carry the cardboard box from the truck. When it was opened, Henry,

Andorra and four other intensely curious people crowded around. The 1x12 base was lifted out by three sets of hands; Henry poked gently at the part of the box Andorra had tried to clean.

"Silver clad cedar, I'd guess. Amazing that it's not all oxidized away. Almost no air down there. How deep was it?"

"Between two and three feet," Andorra reported. "The earth was extremely dry."

"Great. Good work. This menorah looks like the most remarkable artifact of old Jewish culture I've ever seen here. This may be yucca fiber wrapped around it. See these bits here? I'm sure the menorah predates the Conquest, look at the quality of the metal work. See, right here you can make out some engraving. This was probably made in Spain. We'll be able to carbon date the wood and fabric. It definitely would be worth it."

"I've done some research that makes me think my family's land was granted to a Sandoval who came up with Oñate. I'm greatly interested in the age of these things," Andorra said.

"It's a production to do the dating and it'll take a long while, but we'll get right to work on it. I think we can legitimately include this in one of our grants—the dating isn't cheap. I'll keep you informed. Or come in anytime and check out what's happening."

"Great, Henry. If it turns out to be relevant, I can write up my research for your records."

It was nearly two when Andorra left the museum. Sitting on a bench near the courtyard entrance, she looked up toward the hills, inhaling the scent of piñon on the spring air. Next was the visit to Nick's house for the clothes Christina had borrowed. She took a deep breath, found the phone number and dialed.

"*You have reached the home of Nick and Christina White. Please leave a message.*"

Her heart sank.

"Hi, guys. Sorry I missed you. The museum is excited about the chest. They're going to do carbon dating. I'll be in touch about the clothes. The cat misses you, Christina. Me too. Bye."

There it was: The tale of Andorra and Nick. Nobody home.

"Dad, we missed Andorra! She left a message while we were out!" Christina yelled across the courtyard. They had gone to the store, just for a moment, to buy tea for her. The house was neat and the bathrooms cleaned, all ready. Nick had arranged his paintings for her viewing.

"Call her quick!"

"Oooh, her phone must be off," Christina groaned.

Nick sat on his stool and stared into space. Since he'd found out that Christina had run away to Andorra, he couldn't seem to separate them in his mind. He thought of the wonderful day, yesterday, with Christina her sweet self again and the discovery of the chest. How was it that time spent with Andorra was always an adventure? Now she would think they hadn't stayed home to see her. His disappointment was intense.

Andorra had hovered at the edge of his consciousness ever since they had arrived in Santa Fe, but getting Christina settled in school, and having an affair with Sita, had served to dampen the sting of their failure to connect. Sita had been just what he told himself he wanted—pretty, sexy and not interested in commitment. She reserved most of her passion for up-to-the-minute culture, dreaming of becoming a trend spotter in New York and begging Gerard to help her get a job in a gallery there. Her position was that he owed her; he had broken off their affair not long before Nick showed up.

Nick's affair with her also had ended, though this

time it was her idea. "Let's face it, Nick. You're just not that into me," she had said, putting on a cute pout. And he wasn't, though perhaps he should have tried harder; she'd be a loss to the gallery if she went to New York. She sure could sell pictures, and getting her over tonight to take care of the arousal that always accompanied time with Andorra would have been just fine too. But, shit, it wasn't Sita he wanted.

Christina came into the room. "Dad, what are we going to do about Andorra?"

"What do you mean?" he asked, knowing full well what she meant. Christina had been matchmaking ever since they got in the car to come home from La Escondida, first presenting him with a sketch she'd made of Andorra on her porch, and then finding a way to work her into every conversation. If she was trying to be subtle, she had done a pretty bad job of it. Now it looked as though she was coming out in the open.

"Don't you think Andorra is really nice?"

"Of course I do."

"Well, Dad, you need a girlfriend. I think Andorra would be a good one."

"Christina, I'm not sure Andorra is interested in me that way. I think she likes you more than she does me."

"Dad, anyone would like you."

Nick laughed. "Baby, you ran away from me."

Eighteen

Taye came to the Sandoval hacienda after dark and pounded at the bolted double doors until José heard him calling for Don Rodrigo. José refused to open the door, but went quickly to tell of the unusual visit, whispering in Rodrigo's ear as the family sat at a late, and cold, supper. The heavy man glanced sharply at his servant, excused himself courteously to his wife, and left the room. The courtyard was milky pale with starlight as Rodrigo crossed it and unbolted the *zaguán*—the small door within the large ones.

When he returned to his family, he did not take his place at the table but stood in the doorway, fingering his heavy, gray-streaked beard, brow furrowed, eyes fixed on a distant point. At last his wife noticed his preoccupation.

"What is it, *querido?*" Socorro asked. "Why are you standing there? What has happened? Come sit. Eat your food."

He looked at his wife and daughter, imagining the hysteria with which they might receive his information, but he could think of no way to hide it from them, or much mitigate it.

"Taye, from the Pueblo, was at the door. He said—I regret I must tell you—there will be an attack on La Vida at dawn."

"What? Attack?" his wife exclaimed.

"He said that all the Pueblos are going to attack the Spanish tomorrow. All the northern settlements. The priests as well, especially the priests. Perhaps they could come here." Taye had most definitely said that they *would* come to La Escondida, but Rodrigo could not bring himself to tell it. "I think it best if we leave for a time," he said as he began looking quickly around the room, wondering how to deal with their possessions.

"Leave? They are our friends! They are Christians! We have never harmed them," his wife cried, leaping to her feet. Their daughter, Eufemia, let out a shriek and clutched her mother.

"My treasures, it will be best if you ride toward Santa Fé, now, tonight. Likely it will be no more than an

316

adventure, a sleepy one. José! Where are you?" José ran back into the room. "Assemble the household. Everyone." José spun around and ran into the courtyard. They heard him calling for Pablo, María Elena, Abel and Dolores.

Pablo appeared, his pockmarked face anxious, his arms full of firewood for the kitchen, and Rodrigo ordered him to the stables. "Get the horses saddled for the *señoras* and the rest of you."

"Don Rodrigo, what is happening?"

"The Pueblo is planning some disturbance tomorrow."

"A disturbance?" he asked as the others filed into the room.

Rodrigo shot a look to quiet him, but Pablo continued, "You want us to leave the hacienda? Is this not the safest place we could find?"

The servants looked from Pablo, to Don Rodrigo, to Doña Socorro, and back. Dolores quickly crossed to Socorro and Eufemia and put her arms around the girl.

"Listen to me," Rodrigo said, abandoning the idea of minimizing the danger. "Taye has warned me that the Pueblos will rise up tomorrow at dawn to attack the Spanish, wherever they are found. They are many and I will not risk the women. There are soldiers in Santa Fé; we will be safe there if this becomes serious." He turned again to his wife and daughter. "Get into your riding clothes. Pack your valuables. Pablo and José will protect you."

"*They* will protect us! What about you?" his wife cried.

"I will follow shortly. I must go to La Vida and warn my brother. You should go by the river and then through the pass. I will join you."

"Rodrigo, what do you mean 'you will follow?' I am not leaving without you," Socorro exclaimed.

"This must be why Mitsha and Koitsa are not in the kitchen," Rodrigo said as he threw open a large chest and began looking hurriedly through it.

"Rodrigo! Speak to me!" Socorro demanded, tears starting in her eyes.

"My dear, forgive me for alarming you. Likely I am overcautious, but even if the worst is true, we have some time. Taye said the warriors will go first to La Vida, where they will surely be defeated if the town heeds my warning. Also, I cannot leave the stock unattended, but I will ride hard to catch up with you after I take care of these affairs. This is our home and we will return. I swear it."

In no more than an hour, Rodrigo kissed his wife and daughter goodbye. Six horses had been saddled and the five mules were loaded with clothing, valuables and food. Arquebuses, powder and ball were

318

at the ready. Once more charging the men to keep the women safe, cautioning them to ride well to the east of San Gabriel de los Españoles, and warning them to avoid all the other settlements, he promised to follow swiftly. When all were mounted, when tearful goodbyes had been said and God had been exhorted to reunite them promptly, Rodrigo slapped the rump of the lead animal and watched the little company ride into the darkness.

As the hoofbeats faded away, he slowly turned to look at the fortress-like hacienda, built thus with Apache raiders in mind, not the peaceable Pueblo. Should he return from La Vida, drive the livestock inside the walls, stay and defend it, or follow his family as he had promised? He thought of his father, Don Javier, who had died here at La Escondida. What would he have done?

Rodrigo remembered his father and mother's decency and fairness to the Pueblo people and his own attempts to do likewise. He thought of all the years they had been invited to the dances at Heishi; of the boys bringing game and fish for sale, and the purchases of baskets and bowls far exceeding what was needed. He remembered how his Pueblo workers had expanded the hacienda, maintained the barns and the corrals; how Mitsha, or her daughter, had prepared almost every meal for two decades; and how the wages he had paid those workers had made them fat and healthy and well-housed. Perhaps all this had been rewarded tonight.

His family had never insisted on displays of Christian devotion in return for their friendship, like the priests and some of their village neighbors. It could be that they *had* taken comfort in the Pueblo's apparent conversion, but as the keeper of the secrets, Rodrigo's own relationship to Christianity was ambivalent at best. His devotion to the family Sandoval, however, was total. He thought of how he had picked out the family crest, three golden orbs and a scimitar, on the rock near the house, hitting stone on stone, as hard as he could for two days before his father had discovered him and embraced him with approval.

It had been just after his father had shown him the religious objects he had received from his mother and told him of the family history, as far back as he knew it. Back to Granada, where the Sandovals had fought alongside the Christian crown, Ferdinand and Isabella, to expel the Muslim Arabs and Berbers who had conquered Iberia nearly eight hundred years earlier. Back to their cruel reversal of fortune—for no sooner had they been thus used, and rewarded with the right to show the orbs and scimitar on their crest, had come the Edict of Expulsion of 1492 commanding all Jews to leave within four months or be put to death.

The family had become *conversos,* converts to Christianity, and kept their wealth and lands, though, always under suspicion by the Church, they had eventually found it wise to relocate to New Spain. And history had repeated itself there. So they had fled before, Rodrigo thought. They would be prudent and survive again.

He decided he would flee, but vowed to himself to return. The settlers would best these Indians; only surprise could give them the advantage, and this would be over soon. Rodrigo went to the house for the chest and took it to the rock he had made into the Sandoval shrine. Digging quickly, by lantern light, he made a cache for the treasured objects deep in the earth, and covered them carefully. The act was his pledge that he would redeem his inheritance.

The hacienda was silent. With the departure of the household and the cattle scattered to their summer pastures, only the milk cow, her calf, and his horse were left in the barn. The horse would carry him away; the cow and calf he would turn loose to fend for themselves; the poultry as well, though he feared the coyotes would soon find them. When he had dragged the cow out of the barn and done his best to drive her and the calf toward the hills—a task complicated by the dogs' confusion at this strange behavior—he mounted his horse and rode quickly toward La Vida to warn Miguel and all who would listen, calling to the dogs to follow behind.

The next afternoon, the calf and its mother— back in her stall and complaining mightily about her feed—were stolen. The grazing stock, where it could be found, was driven toward the Pueblo, and the hacienda and outbuildings were set ablaze. Sometime in the night, a summer storm found the *vigas* collapsed and smoldering, and began the task of returning the mighty adobe walls to the earth.

~~~~~~~

There. She had tied in her precious new find. Andorra sat back in satisfaction, considering what was next. Eufemia, by then married to her cousin, would return to reclaim the land. It would take over a decade, during which Rodrigo Sandoval would die in bitter disappointment in El Paso, where his father had crossed the Rio del Norte with Oñate.

The Pueblos had only a brief victory. The Spanish had come back and eventually the Americans had followed. Unlike the Plains Indians who claimed tracts too vast for the White Man to tolerate, the Pueblo people had been permitted to keep their cornfields and adobe villages, though many had sunk in hopelessness over the years. The Spanish had seen the village a few ridges away when it stood seven, some said nine, stories high; now it was a pile of rubble on the edge of a meager cluster of houses. But the pride was still alive there, just as the Spanish heritage was still honored and celebrated, just as there were yet a few embers of ancient Jewish identity glowing too.

Now she was determined to make her decisions about Isabel's story. Andorra had started the book with her return to New Mexico, carrying her father's ashes, and had used her own parents' history with few changes. She reread the part about Isabel meeting Ian. She had made him a successful author living in the old Martinez place, writing his fourth book. He was just as beautiful as Nick had been, bathing in the front yard. Andorra fell into reverie as she reread her description of his body. It was no great leap to the memory of him pressing into her. Never mind. Back to work.

Hiking up to the house with her father's ashes, Isabel observes the landscape, the description paralleling what she had written for Javier and Bernabé as they discovered the same country, likewise were caught in the rain, and found the meadow and spring. Isabel and Ian spend the night in the mine, outwit the guys with the meth lab, and bury the ashes. Ian suspects there's another object in the hole, but he won't tell Isabel until later. A good touch.

Was Ian a strong enough name? As strong as Nick? Perhaps he should be Max. Or Mark. Mark—that was good. Ian was too English. Here was a question: should Mark be Jewish? Jewish with the first name of the New Testament writer? Perhaps not. What were the really strong Jewish names? Should he have a Jewish mother waiting for him to marry a good Jewish girl, and would Isabel qualify after the discovery of the menorah? Or was his family not observant, or demanding, but nevertheless delighted by her remote Jewish roots?

She wrote about the conversation in the mine, recalling as best she could what she and Nick had said. She remembered the warmth of the fire and their voices cautiously soft, their pretense of disinterest. She imagined—how about Sam? Yes, Sam was good—she imagined Sam's surreptitious scrutiny of Isabel's body and the arousal he had to conceal.

Isabel then goes off to Mexico to look for records of families that fled the Inquisition, and incidentally, to help rescue Sam's daughter, Ariadne. She and her mother are living in Cuernavaca with a Spaniard from the petty nobility, a true degenerate. Sam and Ariadne are reunited, and in the euphoria of the event, Isabel and Sam have wild, passionate sex.

What if this book got published and Nick read it? Christina too. She could just tell Christina that part wasn't based on reality. It was a romance novel... When exactly had it become a romance novel? Anyway, she had to add some romance, right?

Andorra remembered advising Christina to censor reality if she didn't like it. Hmm. She had better revisit that conversation someday soon, to be sure she wouldn't be responsible for Christina taking some crazy stance regarding truth and fiction.

So, Sam and Isabel agree that they've made a mistake, and despite having gone off like erupting volcanoes, they don't want to see each other anymore. How absurd was that? The scene definitely needed thinking through.

What *had* they said to each other? It had seemed reasonable, necessary, at the time, hadn't it? But Andorra couldn't make the conversation sound sensible except by implying that they were deluding themselves and being hopelessly blind to their own motivations. Fine. She wouldn't keep the poor fools apart much longer.

Shutting off her computer, Andorra left her desk and walked out into the yard to look over the construction site, with the cat as her aloof companion. Weekends were quiet without Pat and the boys banging, laughing and calling her over to make a decision, and though the silence had its charm, how wonderful it had been having Christina here, Andorra thought. The house was clearly too big just for her. Had she been building for more people, unawares? For a family?

Andorra thought about her conviction that motherhood wasn't for her, that the poor parenting she had received from her mother would make bad choices inevitable if she should have children of her own. But what had Christina done but beg for mothering, and what had she done but leap at the challenge with eagerness? Indeed, she loved Christina, little struggling, growing thing. Suddenly, there was no doubt in her mind that she could be a good mother to her. And how could she stand not knowing if her maths grade came up? How could she bear not being near to help her delay acting on her sexuality? And Nick? At once, Andorra knew she loved Nick too. He was handsome, funny, a good father, a wonderful lover, resourceful, talented, smart... Andorra laughed at herself, scooped up the cat and hugged it until it wriggled free.

The partially built rooms looked toward a slope of pines and a scattering of aspens. New grass, in its soft, even growth, gave the landscape the look of a carefully groomed park. This place, her home, was blessed. And she? Her youth had been miserable, but that was over. She'd had a loving father who had left her a rich heritage, and financial independence, and relatives she cherished. Why shouldn't she have a wonderful partner? Fear of mothering had kept her single, but now Christina's need had shown her not only that there was nothing to fear but how dearly she wished to have such experiences in her life. She was certain that all she had to do was to tell Nick, again, that they had made a mistake, and he would immediately agree. If he hesitated she would take him to bed, remind him. Andorra laughed again.

"Hi, sweetie," Andorra said. "I'm coming in to Santa Fe to the museum to see what's happening with the chest. Do you and your dad want to see the laboratory?"

"Sure! I'll ask him. He'll be right back. He went around the corner for some milk. We're so sorry we missed you! We'd gone out to buy you some Earl Grey tea. I told Dad you liked that kind. That's what I drink now too."

"How thoughtful. We had bad timing." Andorra

smiled happily. "So how are you doing? Is it good to be home?"

"I wanted to see you, Andorra."

"Why? Is something wrong?"

"No, it's something pretty good. My boyfriend's parents say he can come over and hang out with me."

"Great! It's a good thing you came back to Santa Fe, right? What's his name anyway?"

"Reese."

"I guess he gets tired of peanut butter jokes."

"Probably he likes me 'cause I never mention peanut butter," Christina laughed. "Oh, here's Dad."

"Your menorah," Henry said, "is made of bronze. Iberian—that is, from Spain. Fourteenth century, I'd say. Here's another thrill. The cloth was wrapped around a mezuzah, *and* a tower, a spice box."

Andorra, Christina and Nick leaned close to see.

"I can't believe it. It's too wonderful," Andorra said. She turned to Christina. "The mezuzah is a little box Jews put on the door frame. It contains a prayer. You touch it each time you enter. I don't know about the spice box."

"I believe the spices are to make a sweet smell as consolation for the Sabbath being over. These are both bronze and have very fine workmanship. You can see these parallel raised areas in the menorah. Those would be the Torah scrolls. I'm guessing it's from Spain too."

"Do you think the spices are still in there?" Andorra asked Henry.

"It seems so. It will be interesting to see where they come from."

"So these must have been carried over by Jews when they came from Spain to Mexico?" Nick suggested.

"I can't picture another scenario. Pretty risky, huh?" Henry said.

"Then these traveled to New Mexico with Jews who came with the Conquistadors?" Christina asked.

"You're well informed! Yeah, they certainly could have. I asked Martin Frank of the Society for Crypto-Judaic Studies to come over to see this. We can't date the metal, but we can the wood, paper and cloth—the organic material. We should get country of origin from the fibers. We have lots of exciting work to do. You know, Andorra, if you want, there's a genetic test that can pick up a marker for the Cohanim, the Jewish priestly class. There's a fairly limited gene pool in these northern New Mexico villages so there's a chance you'd show it."

"I guess my family let their Jewishness slip away,"

The Lives of La Escondida

Andorra sighed. "Sometimes I think my father was trying to tell me after his strokes, but perhaps not. He'd never said anything before. How strange that he led me to the discovery anyway. I think I'll put that mezuzah on my door when you've collected all the information you can. Please don't tell me it's too valuable, Henry."

"It is, but it's yours, and you can do what you want. Umm, maybe best on the inside of the door."

"I can't wait to get back to my book!" Andorra exclaimed. "I've made Rodrigo, Javier's son, bury the chest as he's running from the Pueblo Revolt. That was when the Pueblos coordinated an attack on the Spanish and drove them out of New Mexico for twelve years. Then I have to get the family back to the land. I think Rodrigo's daughter will come back and rebuild in the same place. I'll keep her a Sandoval by having her marry her cousin. I am having so much fun!" Andorra laughed. Then she cocked her head, a thought distancing her eyes.

"Uh, oh. I just thought of something. I said Rodrigo was told by his father, Javier, about the Sandoval family history, and I made up a history and a meaning for the petroglyph too. It's supposedly golden orbs and a scimitar because the family fought the Moors.

I have to make Javier know about this family history so he'll be able to tell his son. Rewriting required. I'll have his grandmother tell him, I suppose. Writing a book is rather like solving a puzzle. Quite interesting and absorbing for me, but possibly tedious for others?"

"But Andorra," Christina said, "his grandmother was on his mother's side, and he has to get that story from his father's side. They both have to know they're Jewish."

Andorra sat straight up. "Christina! You are so right! I was completely missing that. Thank goodness I gave you my book to read! Javier goes on and on to Inez about his *mother's* family but doesn't mention his father's. I'm going to put you in my acknowledgements."

Christina blushed and squirmed in her chair, looking as though it was her birthday, Christmas and all eight days of Hanukkah rolled into one. Nick reached over and gave her shoulder an affectionate push.

They sat in the patio of the Santa Fe house drinking the recently purchased Earl Grey tea. Andorra had thought the house delightful and Nick had let her see his paintings, even those that he had not yet declared finished. The gardens were coming alive with spring; purple and orange irises bloomed in dense clumps; an apricot tree, sheltered from the recent cold snaps, displayed both flowers and tiny, set fruits. The day was slipping toward evening and the magic hour, as only New Mexico could conjure it, was approaching.

"You know," Andorra continued, "I wrote a scene between Javier and his mother where she gives him a religious statue and tells him it contains holy relics."

"That was a good part," Christina said, nodding.

"It's strange. That part I wrote without knowing anything about our discovery, and we have such a small menorah that it might actually have been hidden in a statue. I imagine Javier gives the image to the first church in the village, minus the relics, of course. The priest will be thrilled to have such a fine Old World *santo*. Hmm, I wonder when Javier looks inside? Any ideas you have, Christina, let me know."

Christina giggled.

"Andorra, let me take you to dinner. Bargello? Chef from Tuscany? Just over on Canyon Road? I still owe you for taking such good care of Christina."

"That would be fun but I hate to drive back so late after wine and all."

"We have a guest room. You could stay here," Christina said, leaping up excitedly. "Come on, Andorra, say yes."

"Oh, all right. Are these clothes okay?"

"Absolutely!" Christina gave her father a glance, uttered a loud whoop, and ran off to her room.

"What's got into her?" Andorra asked innocently.

"Beats me."

In the restaurant, fine wood paneling covered the lower third of the walls, and niches above held a collection of antique *santos* whose gilded halos and costume accents glowed in the candlelight. Nick and Andorra sat between a Virgin of Guadalupe and a Santo Niño de Atocha. The room hummed and clinked with diners; Santa Fe knew how to support its restaurants.

"If you can stand any more book talk, there's something I should tell you," Andorra said quietly.

"Sure, let's hear it."

"The book isn't just Javier and his family and their Jewish connections. They're an historical flashback in a contemporary story. There's a girl, Isabel. She comes from London to La Vida—that's what I call Estancia— then up to her father's old house to bury his ashes."

"Sounding familiar." Nick smiled.

"It's pretty much all there, I'm afraid. She meets Sam, a famous *writer*—your identity is fairly safe. They get into the meth lab adventure, and also, he's looking for his daughter, Ariadne, and—"

"Ariadne!"

"Over the top?"

"A bit."

Andorra laughed. "I'll think of another name. Anyway, Isabel and Sam end up in Mexico and get what's-her-name back and Isabel makes discoveries in her research that form the basis of Javier's story. So I thought I should warn you."

"Tell me about Isabel and Sam."

"Well, let's see. They're conflicted characters— adventurous on one hand and scared of life on the other. I can't make sense of why they don't trust each other. Sam is traumatized by losing his child to his ex-wife, but then he gets her back, and Isabel had a crazy upbringing, but I can't see her as damaged as all that."

"So she begins to think she wants to be with Sam? Even though she's told him repeatedly that she doesn't?"

"Yes...but she'd probably be afraid that Sam would reject her. He seems to be attracted to her physically but he goes off for months at a time and doesn't keep in touch."

"Maybe he's afraid she would stand by her rejection. They've both rejected each other, right?"

"Aren't guys supposed to take those chances?

How are they ever going to get girls?"

"Yes, that's the rule. Guys are supposed to risk it," Nick said, smiling at her. Slowly he reached his hand across the table, palm up, a request for hers. She put her hand into his warm grasp. They sat smiling into each other's eyes and neither looked away.

"Andorra, do you want some help with the ending?"

"Yes," she said in a small voice.

"I think it's time for Sam and Isabel to fall into each other's arms." He paused. "Will you come home with me, Andorra? With me and Christina?"

The waiter suddenly appeared at the table. "May I interest you in dessert? We have classic tiramisu, crème brûlée topped with grilled figs in a raspberry reduction, dark choco—"

Andorra stopped her with a raised finger. "I believe we'll have dessert at home."

~~~~~~~

Aaron jumped up from the table and ran through the door when his father's whoop came from the meadow. They met at the barn, and the boy eagerly took charge of the horse as Ephraim, laughing, joking, unpacked the saddle bags and carried the supplies into the house.

"Maria! Look at the *ropa interior* I bought for you!" In a moment, Aaron heard his mother shriek and laugh. He wasn't sure why she would carry on about underwear, but life with his father was always an adventure.

When the chores were done and they had gathered in the kitchen, Ephraim clapped Aaron on the back, his broad smile nearly hidden by his moustache.

"I've done a fine thing today, *hijo.* They got a lot out of me for the land, those Duran, but I know my father would be proud. How it hurt him that his brother had sold that house and field. Eee, he never forgot it. He complained too much. One time my mother took away his dinner and gave it to the dog. She said the food would make him sick if he ate while he was complaining." Ephraim rocked his chair back and laughed his booming laugh, but then grew serious.

"I know it was because my uncle needed the money. He used to follow the sheeps to Colorado, but after his leg was amputated, how was he to support his family? And, worse, my father didn't have enough to buy the land from him. I know that is what hurt him the most. He shouldn't have blamed his brother. Oh, but Tio did manage to spend too much money on drink, even after he couldn't work. He would play the old sad songs on his guitar and sing. I loved to listen to him. 'La Llorona'—he could make the stones weep with her."

The kitchen at La Escondida was full of the smell of green chile pricking sweetly in the air, as Maria stirred the steaming pot of posole on the blue enamel stove. She listened to her husband's story. It was so important to him, the land, and she was happy he could make his dreams real; his sawmill on the edge of La Vida was so prosperous that they now had holdings as large as anyone in the county. Lydia, just starting as a school teacher, would be provided for. Pray God, Reuben would come back from the Pacific and make a good life here.

"And, you, *hijo*," Ephraim continued, "you and your brother and sister must guard this land. I wish my father had the pleasure I feel to leave such a legacy. Believe me, you will feel proud when you can leave land to your children." Ephraim smiled with satisfaction. Aaron thought no one had ever had such a father.

It was Friday and the sun had just set in its slow summer pace. Maria lit the candles.

~~~~~~~

Notes and Acknowledgements

Andorra's research, and my own, relied extensively on *A History of New Mexico* by Gaspar Pérez de Villagrá (1610), translated by Gilberto Espinosa (1933). Two other valuable resources were William Hickling Prescott's *History of the Conquest of Mexico* and *Life in Mexico* by Frances Calderon de la Barca, both published in 1843. Fanny Calderon de la Barca was the English/American wife of the first Spanish ambassador to Mexico following independence in 1810. Her descriptions of aristocratic society shaped those in Andorra's book. Adolph Francis Alphonse Bandelier's novel, *The Delight Makers* (1890), and his scholarly "Documentary History of the Rio Grande Pueblos of New Mexico" (1910) provided material that I used with shocking looseness, such as the relocation of the defunct Heishi Pueblo.

It was from Stanley Crawford's *A Garlic Testament* that I took the explanation of the profound blue of autumnal New Mexico skies and, in thanks for Harvey Freunglass's encouragement, I named Estancia's river after the one in his book, *Cidermaster of Rio*

Oscuro. Thanks also go to Carol Petersen for introducing me to Frosty the Snowman. The poet Gerard Manley Hopkins rivals nature's beauty itself with his verse about goldengroves and aspens, as does Gayle fulwyler Smith's painting on the cover. Lectures and articles by Stanley M. Hordes made me aware of New Mexico's crypto-Judaic traditions and The Society for Crypto-Judaic Studies. Misael Gradilla patiently corrected my Mexican Spanish.

My dear husband, Jonathan Kingson assisted me at every request; Kinari Webb and Thea Callejón, daughters and early readers, gave me encouragement and commentary, as did many friends, among them Ava Eller, Dave Fisher, Sally Janvier and Debra Old. My writers' group, "San Pancho Writers": Nancy Brown, Channing Enders, Ellen Greene and Gail Mitchell, was with me from my first steps. My sister, Mary Alice Herrin, to whom this work is dedicated, inspired my effort. She was a great reader of romances and a sometime resident of New Mexico. When she was terminally ill, I offered her this gift.

About the Author

Carolyn Kingson was born in New Orleans and spent thirty-seven years in a small village in northern New Mexico. She and her husband now live in another small village on the Pacific coast of Mexico.

www.carolynkingson.com

Made in the USA
Charleston, SC
24 February 2012